The Keys of the Kingdom

STANDING IN HOLY PLACES
BOOK FOUR

THE KEYS
OF THE
KINGDOM

BY CHAD DAYBELL

spring creek
BOOK COMPANY
Provo, Utah

ISBN 13: 978-1-932898-91-0
e. 1

Published by:
Spring Creek Book Company
P.O. Box 50355
Provo, Utah 84605-0355

www.springcreekbooks.com

Cover design © Spring Creek Book Company

Printed in the United States of America
Printed on acid-free paper

AUTHOR'S NOTE

Thank you for the support and encouragement you've given me as this series has progressed. I greatly appreciate it!

As the series moves forward to explore the final scenes before the Second Coming of Jesus Christ, I feel the need to emphasize once again that the specific events portrayed in these novels are fictional. I certainly don't claim to know specific details about the future. The characters and storylines have come from my imagination, not through revelation.

Along those lines, some readers have expressed the wish that I had spent more time on certain subplots, such as the journey of the Ten Tribes. I would have loved to do so, but the purpose of the series is to simply give an overall view of what awaits the Saints prior to the Second Coming. I am doing this through three fictional families and the people they meet during their journey through life.

Unfortunately, that means some of the wonderful people and cultures we've met in previous volumes, such as the Guatemalans, the Hopi Indians, or even the Ten Tribes, won't be as prominently mentioned. However, we can be assured that each of these groups will still be busily engaged in the cause of Zion during these exciting times.

Once I have completed the five-volume series, I hope to write additional novels that will explore the lives of these groups and other intriguing characters from the series. I would really enjoy writing first-person accounts from the perspective of Mathoni or

Jeremiah Yakovlevna, but their stories will have to wait until a later time.

I would like to mention that in this volume you'll read more about Kim Brown's sister Tina Marlar who passed away when Kim was a teenager. That storyline is an extension of a novel I wrote in 2003 entitled *Chasing Paradise*. Although that book was originally written as a stand-alone story, in many ways it now serves as a prequel to this series. It's a fun novel that takes place on both sides of the veil, and it provides the background on how Josh and Kim Brown first met. It's still available through many online bookstores at a very good price if you are interested.

As for the future, I truly believe the major events described in this series are going to occur within the next few years, based on the scriptures, the words of the modern prophets, and current world events. The signs of the times that we have been warned to watch for will continue to become more evident as the years pass by.

I think we all have family and friends who scoff a little at the belief that our daily lives are going to change soon, despite the mounting evidence. I have a good friend who is very nonchalant about the future. He has read these novels and thinks they're entertaining, but for some reason he can't imagine these events happening within his lifetime, or even in his young son's lifetime. In some ways I wish he was right, but he's not. I assure you the Savior is not delaying his Second Coming.

The key is to continually follow the teachings of the president of the LDS Church. He is the Savior's mouthpiece, and he will keep the Saints informed and on the right track. If we follow his counsel prayerfully and obediently, we'll find ourselves standing in holy places at the crucial moments in the future.

Chad Daybell
March 2010

TROUBLE ON THE HORIZON

The past year had been a time of peace and progress for the Saints in Zion, including such highlights as the dedication of the New Jerusalem Temple, the return of the Lost Ten Tribes, and the translation and publication of many ancient records. There was a feeling of contentment and joy in the city, and many Saints felt certain their lives would just steadily improve until the Millennium arrived.

However, the members of the First Presidency and the Quorum of the Twelve Apostles knew better. Mitko Petrov's letter from Moscow had reminded them the Coalition was alive and well, despite its internal struggles following World War III. The conflict between Russia and China that had temporarily weakened the Coalition had been resolved and its member countries were united again. Their quest for global domination was back on track, and the leaders wouldn't be satisfied until their two greatest enemies—Israel and America—were conquered and in their control.

The Coalition had recently made great strides to "properly educate" their people by emphasizing science over faith. Organized religion was frowned upon as a potential threat to the group's objectives. Congregations of Christians and Jews were specifically targeted, and those people who continued to openly worship God endured excessive persecution from both their government and their neighbors.

Thankfully the Saints living in Europe and Asia had completed their migration to New Jerusalem during the Russia-China dispute, because the newly unified Coalition would have never allowed such an exodus. The Saints had quietly locked their temples and meetinghouses and left them in the Lord's care. More than three million Saints had crossed the sea to New Orleans and then made the trip up the Mississippi River to St. Louis before settling in New Jerusalem.

Several thousand Saints from South America had also migrated to New Jerusalem, but the governments in that part of the world were barely functioning and didn't interfere in the lives of the people. So the majority of the Saints stayed there and relocated near temple sites to establish Cities of Light, particularly in Colombia, Ecuador, Peru, Chile, Brazil, and Argentina.

Although the Church leaders took seriously the possible threat of another Coalition invasion, they were more concerned with several Biblical prophecies that had yet to be fulfilled. The scriptures speak of worldwide disasters, particularly the seven plagues mentioned in the Book of Revelation that would precede the Second Coming. The leaders knew the Saints wouldn't be completely spared during those events, and they were conscious of the need to prepare the people for these upcoming trials.

At this time, the three main families in this series were continuing to serve in various capacities. As this volume begins:

Tad and Emma North live in New Jerusalem with their children. With the dedication of the New Jerusalem Temple, Tad's assignment as a brick mason working on the temple plaza had come to an end. After a few days of rest, Tad was called to serve as a bishop in an expanding area of New Jerusalem that lacked experienced priesthood leaders. He and Emma soon moved into that ward's boundaries several miles from the city center.

Emma has thrown herself fully into their new assignment and she quickly made friends in their new neighborhood. Tad called her to serve as the ward's Relief Society president to get visiting teaching rolling and to demonstrate to the sisters how to effectively run the organization. In her limited spare time she still helps edit manuscripts as the apostles steadily translate the numerous ancient plates brought to the city by Mathoni and Josh Brown.

The Norths' son David is now 20 and serving as a missionary among the Ten Tribes of Israel in the southern portion of New Jerusalem. He and the other missionaries are having great success. His girlfriend Phyllis, the young woman who came to Zion with the Saints from the Washington D.C. Temple, recently moved from David's grandparents' home into an apartment near the BYU-Zion campus. He hopes she's not dating very much while he's away.

Charles is 16 and attends a high school that focuses on horticulture. He spends much of his time out in the fields learning from master gardeners the best ways to grow fruits and vegetables, and his teachers expect that he'll quickly rise into leadership positions in Zion's food-production network. His fun personality helps him make friends with everyone, and he is fitting right in with the youth in their new ward.

Leah has turned 13, and she's happy to finally be a teenager. She has a talent in dealing with young children, and she's at the top of the list of several young couples when they need a baby-sitter. She has been called as the second counselor in the Beehive class in their new ward.

Doug and Becky Dalton have been living in New Jerusalem since Doug's return from his year-long mission as a member of the 144,000 high priests. He senses he'll be leaving again soon on another mission, but he's hoping he can somehow take his family with him this time. Meanwhile, he's been using his skills as a physical therapist at a downtown clinic, where he treats numerous people each day.

Becky is busy at the elementary school she helped establish in their neighborhood. She was recently asked to serve as the school's vice principal. Justin is now seven and Heather is five, and they are enjoying their gospel-based classes.

Daniel is nearly three years old and attends a special pre-school class at the school. Although he still can't talk, he has learned to stand and can limp along with the help of a small crutch under his arm. He always has a smile on his face and is a great example of perseverance to the other children.

Josh and Kim Brown are still adjusting to Josh's new assignment to serve as an apostle in Israel for the foreseeable future. It came as a shock to them, and they miss each other deeply.

Kim continues to live in their home among the Guatemalan Saints. Their twins, Timothy and Tina, will soon turn two years old. The pair are admittedly mischievous, and Kim devotes most of her time trying to keep them fully clothed and out of the cupboards.

Kim continues to serve as a Family History online data coordinator for the Church as time allows, and this has been a very rewarding calling for her. She tries not to worry too much about Josh, because she knows he's been specifically prepared for his new assignment.

Now on with the story.

CHAPTER 1

———— ✦ ————

Elder Josh Brown scanned the dark water of the Mediterranean Sea through the window of the jet carrying Elder Colton Negus and himself toward the city of Jerusalem. Josh's heart was racing, wondering how the plane could possibly land safely anywhere in Israel. He knew the entire nation was on high alert against a possible invasion, and the odds were good their jet was already being tracked on Israeli radar screens.

Josh turned to glance at Elder Negus, his close friend and a fellow member of the Quorum of Twelve Apostles. They exchanged grim smiles. They were both confident they would live through the next few hours—they just weren't sure how.

"Colton, are you feeling all right?" Josh asked, calling his friend by his first name, which the apostles typically did in non-formal settings.

"No worries," Colton said, nodding toward the door leading to the jet's cockpit. "We're in good hands."

"You're right," Josh responded, trying to let his faith overcome his fears. It was a little easier knowing that John the Revelator was their pilot.

John's small jet had carried them from New Jerusalem to a refueling point in Maryland, then they had refueled overnight on the Canary Islands. From that point, they had stayed over open water as much as possible as they journeyed toward Israel. It was now nearly dawn, and they could see the lights of Israel's coastal cities along the approaching shoreline.

"Elders, come join me," John called from the cockpit. The

5

apostles did so, and they listened intently as John pointed out historical landmarks such as the city of Nazareth nestled in the rolling hills a few miles to the east. He then turned the jet directly south toward Jerusalem.

"These smaller cities aren't as well-armed with anti-aircraft weapons, because the Israelis know that Jerusalem is the main target of their enemies," John said. "But as we get closer to the city, I'm sure they'll be shooting at us. So strap on your parachutes and be ready for anything. When I tell you to jump out the side door, do it."

The apostles were surprised at John's instructions. Colton asked, "Can't we just land the plane somewhere out here in the desert and walk to Jerusalem?"

John shook his head. "The security around Jerusalem is so tight that you'd never get into the city from that far away. I need to get you close enough that you'll be able to parachute inside the city. Just follow my instructions and you'll make it."

The two apostles nodded, left the cockpit and then helped each other put on their parachutes. Josh was really feeling the strain of the past week. The peace and happiness the two apostles had enjoyed with their families in New Jerusalem for the past several months already seemed like a distant memory.

A lump came to Josh's throat as he remembered the prophet calling he and Colton into his office and telling them about the Lord's desire for them to travel to Old Jerusalem, where they would serve for the next few years as the two prophets spoken of in the Book of Revelation.

They were both surprised to receive the assignment, but they humbly accepted it and went home to tell their families. Josh and Kim had stayed up most of the night talking and holding each other close, knowing the importance of the assignment and the fact they would be separated for longer than they had ever been.

The next morning they had traveled with their families to the airport, and the First Presidency was there to bid them farewell. After shaking hands and exchanging best wishes with the Church leaders, Josh had embraced Timothy and Tina for a long time, then held Kim in his arms for even longer.

"I love you," he told her, and she could hardly speak. She simply kissed him solidly and held him tight one more time.

Colton and his wife Cindy had also shared a tender parting kiss, then the couple shared a group hug with their four children.

"You be good for your mother," Colton had told them. "Daddy will be back soon enough."

Then the two apostles had quickly boarded the plane and moved to a window to wave good-bye to their families.

"I guess I shouldn't have told my kids that I'd be seeing them soon," Colton had said. "That wasn't exactly true."

Josh had nodded grimly. "This is definitely a one-way trip."

Once their parachutes were strapped on, the apostles returned to the cockpit to receive further instructions from John.

"We'll be above Jerusalem in about five minutes," John said. "Open the side door and prepare to jump when I tell you to. I'll get as close as I can to the BYU Jerusalem Center. That's the only place you'll be safe right now."

"Where are you going to take the plane?" Josh asked.

"There's a small airport in Africa where I can land it," John said. "You two just be prepared to jump earlier if we start getting fired upon. Even if you parachute, those who are shooting at us should keep their eyes on the plane rather on you. I'll try to keep them distracted so you can make it to the ground safely."

The apostles went to the side door and threw it open. A cold burst of wind lashed at them as they stood in the opening. Both of them had parachuted before, so jumping from the plane didn't necessarily frighten them. They just had no idea of what awaited them when they reached the ground.

Plunk! Ping! Plunk!

Josh looked in terror where three bullets had ripped into the side of the jet only a few feet from where he stood.

"Jump now!" John shouted from the cockpit.

Colton leaped first, followed by Josh. Seconds later they pulled their ripcords and their parachutes blossomed out as the first rays of morning sunlight crept over the horizon. For a brief moment Josh wondered whether they had just opened themselves up as sitting ducks for the enemy sharpshooters, but he looked over his shoulder to see John had pulled the jet into a wild spin that surely kept the attention of the gunmen on the ground.

Within three minutes the apostles landed fifty yards apart in a rock-strewn field. They each received only a few minor bruises as they touched down. Josh stripped off his parachute and ran toward Colton, who had gotten tangled up in his chute.

"Are you all right?" Josh asked.

"Just dandy," Colton replied. "Let's get out of here. I'm sure they'll be looking for us."

Before Josh could reply, John's jet passed over them once more, this time with flames erupting from the tail. The jet nose-dived into a small knoll close by, shaking the ground and knocking the apostles to their knees.

Before they could even get to their feet, John was standing next to them. His clothes were charred and smoking, and he had an intense look on his face.

"That sure didn't go as planned, but we're still okay," John said. "We need to get moving, though. The Israeli soldiers will be here soon looking for you."

"Aren't they the good guys?" Colton asked. "Don't we want them to find us?"

"Eventually, but not under these circumstances," John said. "At the moment you're unauthorized intruders. Let's get you someplace safe. There's an abandoned farmhouse over this hill."

CHAPTER 2

When the apostles reached the farmhouse, John guided them to a set of stairs behind the building that led down to a small door.

"The Israelis will surely search this farmhouse, but behind this door is a root cellar," John said as he pulled it open. "Go in as far as you can and cover yourselves. I'll close the door behind you."

Cobwebs filled the entrance and a damp, unhealthy smell wafted from the darkness, but the faint sound of an approaching helicopter helped propel them into the cavern. The apostles crawled several feet inside and then covered themselves with a piece of rotted canvas.

"See you soon," John said as he slammed the door shut.

Within a minute the helicopter landed near the house, and while the engine wound down, the apostles could hear the floorboards creaking as several soldiers entered the home and searched each room.

"They have to be here," one man shouted. "There's nowhere else they could have gone. Check the back."

The apostles hardly dared to breathe as a man came partway down the cellar stairs and yanked on the door handle, but it didn't move. He tried it again without success, then turned back. He entered the house and told his commander, "There's nowhere to hide back there—just an old stairway filled with weeds that probably leads to a cellar. It hasn't been used in years. I couldn't even get the door to budge."

Josh sighed with relief. John must have wedged the door shut somehow. The apostles listened intently as the soldiers left the house. The Israeli leader stood on the front porch and shouted, "This is your last chance to come out. We located your parachutes and know this is the only place you could be hiding."

The soldiers then went silent, listening for any hint of the parachutists, but Josh and Colton didn't move a muscle. Finally the leaders said, "Let's get out of here, but leave them a gift, okay?"

One of the men laughed and could be heard walking back into the house. Then he hurried out as the helicopter started up again. As it took off and moved away into the distance, Colton whispered, "Do you think we're safe to—"

BOOM!

An explosion rocked the building, sending debris crashing down on them.

As the dust settled, Colton groaned loudly.

"Are you hurt?" Josh cried out.

Colton groaned again and said, "I got knocked on the noggin, but I'll be fine."

The explosion had ripped the house apart, and the morning sunlight streamed down on them through the jumbled mess of bricks and boards above them. "That bomb must have been the 'gift' the soldier left for us," Josh said.

Suddenly the cellar door was ripped open, and the apostles could see John peering in. "How are you two doing?" he asked.

"We're okay," Colton replied, looking closely at John, who had changed out of his charred clothing into a threadbare outfit a street beggar might wear.

"Why the fancy clothes?" Colton asked.

"I want to look as inconspicuous as possible," John said. "The Israelis shot down the plane sooner than I'd hoped, and we're still several miles outside of Jerusalem. Come out of there and I'll show you how we're going to get you into the city."

The apostles carefully climbed through the rubble and found John standing next to what could only be called a large tricycle. It had a small flatbed between the rear tires to carry items, and it was filled with small cardboard boxes and blankets.

"With all of the heightened security around Jerusalem, this is the only way we'll be able to get you past the guard at the gate. Lay down under the blankets, and I'll cover you with boxes. I'll be taking some back roads, and we should get there within a couple of hours."

Josh and Colton saw they didn't really have much of a choice, so they climbed into the back of the tricycle and lay down as John carefully packed the boxes on top of them.

"Ahh, the life of luxury," Colton said.

Soon John was pedaling furiously toward Jerusalem, and as a translated being he made tremendous time along the narrow paved roads. Meanwhile, the exhausted apostles drifted off to sleep to the steady sound of the squeaking tricycle tires.

When they finally reached a checkpoint into the city, John whispered to the apostles, "It's time to wake up, but don't make a sound."

Within seconds the tricycle came to a stop and the apostles lay motionless as John talked to one of the checkpoint guards. The man was very reluctant to let John through the gate.

"I'm sorry, but since you don't have any identification, I can't let you through," the guard told him.

"Sir, with all due respect, you must be new here," John said. "I've passed through this gate for many years without any question."

"I'm sure that's true," the guard said, "but we've had to really tighten our security lately."

"I completely understand, but hopefully we can work something out," John replied. "On my previous stops here, I've given the guard a few apples to show my appreciation for his hard work. Maybe I can do even better for you."

John reached into the bed of the tricycle and pulled out a cardboard box near Josh's feet. "Here you go, sir. I'm going to hand you this entire box of delicious apples and you can just look the other way as I pass through."

The guard took the box in his arms but said, "I don't know if I feel good—"

"Thank you!" John said, cutting him off as he pushed the tricycle through the gate. The guard simply watched him peddle away before finally setting the box down and picking out a nice apple to munch on.

Once they were out of the guard's earshot, Colton called out from under a blanket, "That was mighty brave of you. You handled it well."

John laughed. "I wasn't too worried. What was he going to do? Even if he'd shot me in the back, I would've just kept peddling."

John pulled up to one of the gates leading to the BYU Jerusalem Center, a beautiful eight-level structure on Mount Scopus overlooking the Mount of Olives and the Old City. It had been dedicated in 1984, and for many years BYU professors and students lived there as they studied the Holy Land and took field trips to historical sites. But now the building sat empty and the formerly well-landscaped gardens were overgrown.

"I'm guessing no one lives here anymore," Colton said.

"You're right," John said. "The Church leaders were prompted to remove all faculty and students from Israel just prior to the Coalition invasion. After they left, I sealed up all of the entrances and have kept an eye on the building since then. Now it's your new home."

John unlocked a door and led them inside a dormitory room. "You'll share this room. I've stocked the kitchen with plenty of food and water, so you won't need to worry about that."

Josh went into the dorm room and opened a sliding glass door on the far side. He stepped out onto a patio that had a superb view of the Old City, with the Dome of the Rock clearly visible.

"It's hard to beat the scenery," he said.

John gave them a short tour of the rest of the building, and then they went outside as darkness started to fall. John pointed to an ancient olive tree standing near the main entrance.

"That tree is nearly as old as I am," John said. "I've often thought of it as a great symbol of Jerusalem itself, where three of the earth's major religions—Judaism, Islam, and Christianity—have mingled together over the centuries. Somehow the city has survived through all of their conflicts, and now you two will witness the final outcome."

"I'm glad you mentioned that," Colton said. "I realize we're here to help protect Israel, but where exactly do we start?"

John smiled and motioned toward the city. "We need to go meet with someone who can provide those answers. I'm sorry to make you do it, but hop back into the bed of the tricycle and stay hidden. I promise that after this meeting, you'll be able to travel more openly."

After traveling a few miles, John parked outside an ancient two-story building in the Old City and helped the apostles climb out from under the blankets and boxes.

"Did you see any Israeli soldiers?" Josh asked.

"I only got a few strange looks from people," John responded. "I'm not worried about us being followed."

John led them to the front door and gave a unique knock. After nearly a minute the door opened slightly, revealing a short middle-aged man dressed in the clothing of orthodox Judaism with a white shirt, black pants, and a jacket. When he saw John, a smile spread across his face.

"I'm glad you're back, my dear friend," the man said. "I was starting to worry about you."

"I'm glad to be back," John said, before motioning toward the apostles. "Benjamin, these are my friends from America I've been telling you about."

"Welcome," Benjamin said, beckoning for them to enter. He then led them up a flight of stairs into a large room filled with books and maps. John was happy to see Benjamin Cohen again. It had been several weeks since they had last met, but John had been watching over Benjamin since he was a young boy, much as he had watched over Jeremiah Yakovlevna of the Ten Tribes. Benjamin was a direct descendant of Levi—and therefore an heir to the Aaronic Priesthood—and he would play a key role in Jerusalem's future.

Benjamin invited his guests to take a seat on a couch, and he pulled up a wooden chair in front of them.

"At long last, the Americans have arrived," Benjamin said contentedly. "John has been hinting for several months now that you would come to assist us. Tell me about yourselves."

Josh and Colton each gave brief explanations about who they were, and Josh concluded by explaining they were members of the Quorum of the Twelve Apostles of The Church of Jesus Christ of Latter-day Saints.

Benjamin nodded. "I have a great respect for your church. I visited many times with your professors from BYU, and I understand your history. More importantly, I understand that we need to work together to accomplish our goals."

"We would like that very much," Josh said. "The amazing thing to me is how you have been able to maintain your country, despite the constant threat from other nations."

"As I'm sure you can understand, we have God to thank for that," Benjamin said. "But I do believe this little nation still has a great destiny, as our ancient prophets outlined in their writings. The countries of the Coalition have us surrounded and under siege, but we keep holding on. Our armed forces have performed admirably during our seemingly endless skirmishes with our neighbors."

"How have you been able to do that?" Colton asked. "Haven't they cut off all of your outside resources?"

"Yes, but we're very self-sufficient," Benjamin replied. "Solar power has been widely used in Israel for several years, and this has been essential for our survival. Also, we've had just enough rain to keep our farms operating and raise our own food. So our people aren't starving, although they aren't eating lavishly, either."

At Colton's request, Benjamin then gave the apostles a brief explanation about the troubled history of his people, especially their persecution during the Holocaust in World War II that led to the deaths of six million Jews at the hands of the Nazis.

"All four of my grandparents were killed in the gas chambers," Benjamin said. "It completely destroyed our family, but it didn't extinguish our faith in God. We just pushed forward."

Benjamin then told them about the formation of Israel as a country in the late 1940s, which was a miracle in itself. But since that time, Israel had never experienced peace. There were clashes with surrounding countries in the 1960s and 1970s followed by the Palestinian Liberation Organization's efforts to topple them. Then as the War on Terror escalated and Israel's friendship with the United States became more established, the Arab countries such as Iran and Iraq took turns tormenting the country.

Yet even after the United States fell into chaos and disintegrated during the Coalition invasion, Israel held strong in maintaining its borders and fending off its enemies. In many ways, the country had been largely unaffected by the worldwide upheaval happening around them. The Knesset—the country's 120-member legislature—was intact, and the prime minister still fulfilled his role.

Benjamin said the nation's military, known as the Israel Defense Forces, continued to function, and young Israelis were still being drafted at age 18, with men serving for three years and women for two. This military service created a deep sense of loyalty among the nation's citizens.

Josh and Colton absorbed everything that Benjamin was telling them, but for Colton one detail seemed to be missing. He asked, "So is everyone in Israel of Jewish descent? There seems to be plenty of Muslim and Christian buildings here as well."

Benjamin shook his head. "I'm sorry if I gave that impression. Until this latest siege, Israel has been about 80 percent Jewish, while Muslims constituted about 15 percent of the population. Only two percent of Israelis are Christian, although we obviously still maintain a significant Christian presence and flavor."

"What do you mean by 'until this latest siege'?" Josh asked.

Benjamin held up his hands. "Most of the Muslims have left

the country in the past few months at the invitation of our Arab neighbors, and I can't blame them. There are well-founded rumors circulating that the Iranian leaders are pushing the Coalition to wipe us off the map."

Josh nodded grimly. "That's what we've heard as well, but let's not forget that God is still part of this equation. I know you have plans to rebuild the temple. Is that still progressing?"

Benjamin gave John a questioning look, and John said, "You can trust them. They're on your side."

Benjamin looked relieved. "Yes, we expect to fulfill the prophecy to rebuild the holy temple on the Temple Mount, as outlined by the ancient prophets. We already have the stones stored away, cut to the precise measurements outlined by Ezekiel."

"That's wonderful!" Josh said. "Of course, there's one small problem, right?"

"Yes, the prophecies and our traditions indicate we must build the temple in a certain spot—on the same location of the holy Muslim shrine known as the Dome of the Rock."

Colton shook his head. "Whoa! That's a *big* problem."

"Absolutely," Benjamin said. "The Muslims have long been aware of our intentions, so any related action on our part will spark a holy war of epic proportions."

"What can you do?" Colton asked.

Benjamin shrugged. "As Elder Brown said, it's really in God's hands. But we're hopeful that Elias will be able to help us resolve the problem."

Josh's ears perked up. "Did you say Elias? You mean Elias of Syria?"

Benjamin grinned. "Yes, that Elias. He really is extraordinary. Without him on our side, we may have been destroyed already."

Josh was genuinely astonished that Benjamin was acquainted with Elias of Syria, a peace-loving, captivating man who had emerged out of nowhere two years before the Coalition attack to become a worldwide sensation for his message of global harmony.

"Where is he?" Josh asked. "Has he been here in Israel?"

"He's been visiting here for a few days," Benjamin said. "In fact, I'll be meeting with him tomorrow morning at ten o'clock, and it might be good for all of us to get acquainted. Would you like to join us?"

"Definitely," Josh said with a sense of excitement. He looked over at Colton, who seemed baffled by Josh's sudden interest in this Elias. Colton had lived in England until shortly before the Coalition invasion and therefore had missed out on the media furor in America that had surrounded Elias.

"Don't worry," Josh told him. "I'll explain everything to you tonight."

CHAPTER 3

As the two apostles concluded their meeting with Benjamin Cohen and were returning for their first night in the Jerusalem Center, the extended Dalton family sat together halfway around the world in Mark and Michelle Dalton's front room. It was a sunny Sunday morning in New Jerusalem, but there was a hint of change in the air. The prophet had canceled all Sunday meetings throughout the city and was going to address the Saints via the Church's internet network. Mark had his computer linked to the broadcast, which would begin in a couple of minutes.

Mark looked over at his smiling son-in-law Tad North, a new bishop in a ward of recent converts who were sent to Zion by the 144,000 high priests. This calling had required Tad and Emma to move their family from their cozy home within a few blocks of the temple, but they were excited about the opportunity.

"Congratulations once again on your new calling," Mark said to Tad. "I know you could've stayed home and taken care of some ward business, but thanks for coming."

"Glad to be here," Tad said. "I sense the prophet has something to say that could affect the whole family, so it's good we're all together to hear it."

The computer screen changed to a live broadcast inside the New Jerusalem Temple's central dome. Mark held up his hands and said to the group, "Okay, it looks like we're ready to begin."

The family settled down and focused on the screen. Soon the prophet stepped to the podium and began his address.

"My wonderful Saints, first of all I want to thank you for your faithfulness in all aspects of your lives. New Jerusalem has flourished and is a marvel to behold. In some ways it is hard to imagine the Millennium being more wonderful than the Zion society we're living in. But . . ."

The prophet paused and smiled, glancing over at one of his counselors before saying, "But there is still much work to be done. A few nights ago I was privileged to be shown a vision of North and South America. Not surprisingly, nearly all of the cities are uninhabited and in bad shape. Office buildings and homes are empty and falling apart. Tall weeds now grow where our beautiful parks once were. It was heart-breaking to see these cities in ruin."

The prophet then looked directly into the camera and said, "As I beheld this vision, I told myself, 'This isn't right. We must restore these cities before the Savior comes again.' Then a quote given by the Prophet Joseph Smith in April 1844 shortly before his death came to my mind. He said:

"The whole of North and South America is Zion. The mountain of the Lord's house is in the center of North and South America. When the house is done, the baptismal font erected and finished, and the worthy are washed, anointed, endowed, and ordained kings and priests . . . then the elders are to go through all America and build up churches, until all Zion is built up. But they are not to commence to do this until the temple is built up here and the elders endowed. Then go forth and accomplish the work and build up stakes in all of North and South America."

The prophet continued, "I believe that admonition was partially fulfilled by previous generations, but it could not be completely fulfilled until this time, now that Zion's centerplace has been established and this temple built. *We* are the ones who will now fulfill it."

The prophet got a little choked up at that statement. He cleared his throat and added, "The fulfillment of Joseph Smith's statement will begin by asking those of you who previously lived in certain areas of Idaho and Utah to return to your former homes. I know in some ways this will be almost as big of a challenge as coming to Zion was. But the Lord has cleansed the land of evildoers, and I know we have thousands of capable Saints right here in this city who could make these areas blossom again. Our maintenance missionaries in the Rocky Mountains have evaluated each city and notified us of the ones that are most ready to be rebuilt."

The prophet then lifted a paper and began to read. "They are: Rexburg, Idaho Falls, Pocatello, Logan, Brigham City, Ogden, Bountiful, Salt Lake City, Draper . . ."

Mark glanced over at Doug. It was clear the prophet was reading a list of cities from north to south, and they knew Springville would be coming up soon.

". . . American Fork, Provo, Springville, Spanish Fork, Payson, Nephi, and Manti. Additional cities both in and outside of the Rocky Mountains will be added to this list in the spring."

Mark and Doug grinned at each other. They both felt a surge of excitement to participate in the rebuilding process.

The prophet lowered the list and said, "I specifically invite families who lived in these cities to return to them, but I encourage anyone else who feels inspired to help with this rebuilding process to follow those promptings. The members of the 144,000 and their families will be heavily involved in this process, but we will also need people with a variety of skills to complete this task. I ask you to pray and follow the Spirit in making your decision."

The prophet concluded, "This effort will be coordinated through each ward, so please let your bishop know if you intend to return to your former home. Thank you again for all you do to make Zion such a wonderful place. I testify the Savior is leading this work and guiding us in each of these decisions as we move ever closer to the Millennium."

As Mark turned off the computer screen, he said to his son, "The prophet mentioned the 144,000 would be participating. So did you already know about this?"

"Yes, I was informed yesterday. I've been asked to return to

Springville with my family," Doug said. "Sorry to keep a secret, but Becky and I weren't supposed to tell anyone until now."

"That's fine," Mark said. "I'm sure the First Presidency wanted to keep the gossip to a minimum. But do you have any additional details you could share with us?"

"With winter coming soon, the Church isn't wasting any time," Doug said. "We'll have convoys of Saints departing for these cities within two weeks."

His mother Michelle asked, "How would we get there? Do we have to walk?"

"No, the Church will transport us there in solar-powered buses, and food will be transported to us in trucks until we can live off our gardens and everything is operating smoothly again."

"I don't understand why we don't wait until spring," Michelle said.

"I know how you feel, but the prophet said he feels an urgency about it," Doug said. "That's why we're only rebuilding a few main cities right now, though. That way the Saints here in New Jerusalem will be able to provide food for us until next year. Elder Smith of the Quorum of the Twelve Apostles will be moving to Salt Lake City, and I'll be working under his direction. If we can get a good mix of people—electricians, carpenters, plumbers—we'll get these communities fully functioning in a short time."

"You're right," Mark said. "Now that Sherem's army has been eliminated, it makes sense for us to rebuild the Wasatch Front."

Amid this conversation, the Norths had been silent and looked a little downcast. Tad finally said, "This sounds like a great experience, but with my new calling, I know the Lord wants us to live here for now."

"I agree with Tad," Emma added. "We'll be staying here. Besides, David will probably be returning from his mission soon. It sounds like enough members of the tribes have been converted to the gospel that they can now teach each other. We expect he'll return for his sophomore year at BYU-Zion and continue dating Phyllis."

Emma then looked at her parents and asked, "Do you think you'll go? It kind of sounds like a split decision."

Mark started to respond, but Michelle quickly said, "We'll have to think about it. The prophet asked us to pray about it, and that's what I plan to do."

Mark looked a little surprised at his wife's remark. For him it wasn't even a question. He was admittedly feeling a little restless in Zion. He had loved their assignment to help the Ute tribe bring the sacred gold to Zion, and while he enjoyed serving as an ordinance worker in the temple each afternoon, the thought of helping rebuild Utah really excited him.

"I guess we'll need to talk about it," Mark said carefully.

Michelle gave him a stern look. "Just last week the doctor told you it was time to take it easy and slow down. How does restoring a city fit into that?"

Doug and Emma smiled across the room at each other, enjoying their parents' little spat. Mark noticed the smiles on his children's faces, and all three of them knew there wasn't any point in arguing about it. Michelle needed to work it out in her own mind first, then a decision could be made.

"We'll let you know what our plans are later on," Mark told the group. "The decision is pretty clear for the rest of you, but Grandma is right. We need to pray about it and get a confirmation from the Lord about what we should do."

Emma's daughter Leah leaned over to her cousin Justin and whispered loudly, "I think that means Grandpa's ready for us all to go home."

Everyone laughed, but Leah was correct. After everyone gave hugs and pats on the back, Mark and Michelle soon found themselves standing alone in the living room.

"I'm just a little flustered," Michelle said. "You know how much I hate to make changes. We're heading into winter, and that frightens me a little. All I ever wanted to do is settle down in one place. Now after all of these years of turmoil, I thought we had finally reached that point."

"I know what you mean," Mark said. "Sometimes it feels like these calls to serve in the kingdom won't end until we take our last breath. I don't think the callings will stop then either, but at least the aches and pains will be gone."

Michelle smiled. "I really don't mean to complain, but I admit it was hard on me when Emma and Tad were asked to move. I loved having them here on the same block. I know they're only a few miles away now, but it already feels like a hundred."

"I know what you mean," Mark said. "I miss them too. That's partly why I want to go to Springville. I'm sure we would live close to Doug and Becky. If we stay here, we might not see much of either of our children."

Michelle's eyes got a little misty. "I'm just a little frustrated. I really thought that the one place I'd get to settle down with my kids and grandkids nearby would be in New Jerusalem."

Mark put his arm around her shoulders. "I know exactly what you mean. But let's do what you suggested and pray about it. Maybe I've been a little hasty. I need a confirmation from the Lord as much as you do."

They knelt down next to their couch and held hands, then each one took a turn offering a heartfelt prayer. During Mark's prayer he indicated his desire to return to Utah, and suddenly a rush of the Spirit poured over both of them. Michelle felt it strongly, but she took her turn at praying as well.

"Dear Father, I'm grateful for all of our many blessings, but my desire is to stay in Zion and build up the kingdom here."

She paused, and she waited the Spirit to confirm her decision. She didn't feel anything one way or the other, as if the Spirit was saying, "Either choice is a good option, but you've already received your answer."

Michelle looked over at her husband, but he remained still with his eyes closed and head bowed. She bowed her head again and said, "Father, I'm nervous about what might happen to us in Utah, but I'm willing to go."

The Spirit then filled her heart, and she knew what the Lord's plans were for them. She opened her eyes and whispered, "I guess we'll be moving."

They were soon sitting together on the couch, holding each other close. "I do feel good about going to Utah," Mark finally said. "I know most of the Saints who are our age would be content to stay here and leave this adventure to the younger generation, but I'm eager to help rebuild the city we love. Besides, I've really missed the mountains."

Michelle patted her husband's arm. "Don't worry. I'll be okay. It will be good for me to be near Doug and Becky and the kids. I can take care of Daniel if Becky is asked to help get the school running again. Besides, I'm sure we can come back and visit Emma and Tad once in a while."

CHAPTER 4

Back in Israel, the two apostles had returned safely to the BYU Jerusalem Center and prepared dinner for themselves. As they sat at their table and began to eat, Colton said, "All right, now tell me about this Elias fellow. Do you think he plays a role in why we're here?"

"I really do," Josh said. "Elias has actually been on my radar for several years. When I was serving as a stake president in Nebraska, he started to gain national attention for some prophecies he had made that came true, and for performing so-called miracles. I remember watching a lengthy interview with him on the TV show *60 Minutes,* and afterward I was admittedly as charmed by him as everyone else."

"Well, even if he's a good man, he obviously can't be a prophet of the Lord," Colton said.

"That was my dilemma. As the stake president, I naturally had members asking about whether Elias was a prophet. I told them he seemed to speak the truth, but that the Lord only has one authorized mouthpiece on earth at a time—the president of the LDS Church."

"Exactly," Colton said. "But where did he come from? Did you check into his past?"

"I did," Josh said. "In many ways, Elias' life has a Cinderella feel to it. He was born in poverty in Damascus, Syria, but even as a boy his radiant personality and unusual gifts had gained the attention of many people. When he was a teenager a Syrian businessman sent him to Columbia University in New York City to get an education. The businessman's intent was that Elias would return to Syria after graduation and become a leader there, but while he was in New York, he started making those prophetic statements, and his fellow college students rallied around him. He proclaimed himself a vegetarian and celibate, and he said he was on earth to prepare the way for a 'great change' that was coming. He really caught the media's attention when he moved into a large tent in Central Park, where thousands of his followers would go to hear his latest sermons. Once he started living in the tent, he dressed only in robes and sandals, which added to his mystique."

"He was actually living in the park?" Colton asked. "I didn't know you could do that."

"The city officials did try to kick him out, but his followers staged a sit-in and wouldn't let the police even get near him. Naturally the media quickly latched onto the story, and soon Elias was as recognizable as other single-name celebrities, such as Shaq, Madonna, or Beyonce. You could simply say the name Elias and everyone knew who you were talking about."

"Wow, this guy must be very charismatic," Colton said.

"He is, and he's also a bit of a showman," Josh reflected. "At the time, members of the media were comparing Elias' physical traits to that of New York Yankees' baseball star Alex Rodriguez. Even though Alex was older and reaching the end of his playing career, the two shared the same tall muscular build, olive skin, and powerful smile. It was uncanny, and the late-night comedians had a heyday comparing photos of the two of them. They even both had green eyes. The only difference was the length of their hair, with Elias' ponytail reaching down past his shoulders compared to A-Rod's close-cropped trim.

"The New York tabloids even started calling Elias by the nicknames 'El-Rod' and 'Humble-Rod.' That didn't sit well with A-Rod, who sniped at Elias in the media for a couple of weeks with comments like, 'When that holy man can hit a fastball out of the ballpark, then he can be compared to me.'"

"How did Elias respond?" Colton asked.

"All Elias would say was, 'May God bless Alex's troubled soul,' which only made A-Rod even angrier. The Yankees were in a tight race that season to make the playoffs, and finally the team's manager publicly told A-Rod to shut up and focus on baseball. It was completely bizarre but utterly fascinating at the same time."

"How ridiculous," Colton said. "I don't understand you Americans sometimes."

"I know what you mean," Josh said. "The country was starting to fall apart, but this was what everyone was talking about. Then Donald Trump arranged for a nationally televised meeting between the two of them at Yankee Stadium. Elias even agreed to take some batting practice with A-Rod, and when Elias hit a home run in his robe and sandals, the media went wild, proclaiming it 'The Miracle in the Bronx.'"

"Yes, I remember hearing something about it even in England," Colton said. "I didn't realize this was the same man, though."

"Yep, that's him. Anyway, what bothered me was that Elias was beginning to be compared to Jesus, and it felt completely blasphemous to me. I really started to get bothered when several of the bishops in my stake reported that many Church members were following Elias very closely and some were even basing their daily decisions on his prophecies."

"Whoa, that's not right," Colton said. "I hope you set them straight."

"I did, but while all this was going on, Elias suddenly announced he would be visiting college campuses across the United States, including a stop at the University of Nebraska's basketball arena. I felt compelled to attend and see what this was all about. The stadium was packed with more than 15,000 people, and it had the feel of a Pentecostal revival, with loud music and people swooning in the audience before Elias even came on stage. The media called it 'The Elias Effect.' At these events, everyone seemed to go into a spiritual frenzy, but Elias himself would stay completely calm."

"How did you feel during his speech?" Colton asked.

"I felt strangely at peace, but I also felt the need to actually speak to him," Josh said. "Elias would always greet people after his speeches, so I got in line before the speech was over. After an hour wait, I finally found myself face to face with him. I told him I was a local leader of the Church of Jesus Christ of Latter-day Saints, and that many members of our congregations were starting to follow him."

"How did he respond to that?" Colton asked.

"He slowly shook his head and said, 'That isn't my intention. I don't want to start a religion. My only desire is to spread compassion and understanding among the human race. We all come from different backgrounds and viewpoints, but we're all children of the same Creator. It's understandable that we'll squabble at times, but in the end we should love each other and look out for each other. If we can get along, our potential is limitless.'"

"It sounds like he's on the right track," Colton said. "But what did you feel when you looked him in the eyes?"

"I sensed I was talking to an honest man," Josh said. "He has those large green eyes, and it seemed like I could look deep into his soul. After talking with him, I think he's the real deal. Like I said, I don't know how he fits into the overall plan, but he definitely has a role in it."

Colton nodded. "But how did he end up here in Jerusalem? That seems strange."

"Not really," Josh said. "As I said, I kept track of him pretty closely after that, and just before the invasion he abruptly left the United States and made a pilgrimage back to Syria, where he was greeted as a returning hero and honored son. He became a close confidant to Syria's president, and he was a key figure in peace talks between Syria and Israel. Some people called him a modern-day King Solomon because of his ability to wisely solve problems that no one else could."

"Then why would he be in Israel, though?"

"I'm not sure," Josh replied. "Benjamin had mentioned Elias was somehow protecting the country from being destroyed. I guess we'll find out tomorrow."

✤ ✤ ✤

The next morning the apostles returned to Benjamin Cohen's residence and found that Elias and two companions had already arrived. They shook hands with Elias and introduced themselves.

"Thank you for always emphasizing unity and peace," Josh added. "You've been a positive influence on many people."

"I appreciate your kind words, Elder Brown. I believe we once met at the University of Nebraska a few years ago. Correct?"

Josh was stunned that Elias would remember their meeting. "Yes, that's right. How did you—"

"I never forget a face," Elias interrupted with a smile. "I suppose you're still a leader in the LDS Church."

"I am. We're actually apostles in the Church. Elder Negus and I have been assigned to stay here in Jerusalem."

Elias raised his eyebrows in surprise. "Apostles? Like the ones Jesus Christ had? That's very interesting."

Over the next few minutes, the conversation turned to Israel's status and how they were all in agreement that the country must be preserved, despite the threat from the Coalition forces. Then Elias said to Benjamin, "That's the main reason for my visit this morning. I need to tell you I'll be leaving Israel this afternoon."

"Where will you go?" Benjamin asked, a bit disturbed by the news.

"First back to Syria, and then possibly to other destinations," Elias said. "But I want to thank you so much for the information you've given me. I won't share it with anyone, and it will help me in future negotiations as I seek to keep Israel safe from harm."

"Thank you," Benjamin said. "It's been a blessing to have you here with us. I must admit I'm fearful of what might happen when the other nations know you've left."

Elias shook his head. "You'll be safe. Besides, you now have these apostles here to assist you."

Colton detected a hint of sarcasm in Elias' response. He looked over at Josh to see his reaction, but his fellow apostle was still seemingly mesmerized by the man. They soon all stood and shook hands again. Josh asked Elias, "You're still seeking to achieve world peace and unity, right?"

Elias grinned and clasped Josh's shoulder. "Of course. That's the whole purpose of my life."

Within seconds Elias and his companions had departed, and Benjamin was clearly bothered. "That's not good news at all," he said. "I was hoping he would stay a lot longer. We could be very vulnerable now."

"I agree," Josh told him, "but we also have God on our side. I firmly believe that."

After another few minutes of discussions with Benjamin about how they could work together to protect Israel, the apostles began walking back to the BYU Jerusalem Center.

"Elias certainly has a powerful personality," Colton said, looking sideways at his fellow apostle. "Let's hope he keeps Israel's safety as a top priority."

Josh seemed withdrawn and didn't respond.

"Hey, what's wrong?" Colton asked.

Josh shook his head. "Maybe it's just me, but when I looked into his eyes this morning, something was . . . different."

"In what way?"

Josh stammered a little, trying to put it into words. "It wasn't necessarily a darkness within him, but more of a worldliness and arrogance. The younger Elias I met in Nebraska had the innocence of a baby fawn, but the man we met today didn't have that same countenance. Frankly, it makes me a little nervous."

CHAPTER 5

Nearly a thousand miles to the northeast of Jerusalem, Mitko Petrov anxiously ran his hands through his hair. A Coalition guard was now leading him out of the Kremlin prison cell in Moscow, Russia that had been his home for the past two weeks.

The guard led him to a small bathroom and pointed to a set of new clothing and a shaving razor on a shelf. "Clean yourself up," the guard commanded. "The council wants you to attend their meeting this morning. I'll be waiting outside."

Mitko closed the door and looked in the mirror. His own appearance frightened him a little, but following a shower and a shave, he felt like a new man. He exited the bathroom and was escorted directly to the council chambers.

The leaders of the Coalition nations barely acknowledged his entrance as they talked among themselves, and Mitko was instructed to take a seat near the back of the chambers. There were many more leaders in the room than at the previous meeting when he had first arrived at the Kremlin.

As Mitko sat there, he realized he'd been blessed with the gift of interpretation of tongues. The council heavily relied on translators to help the leaders converse, but Mitko could understand what was being said even before the translation was given.

"Heavenly Father, thank thee for granting me that gift," he silently prayed. "If I'm called upon to speak, please guide me in everything I say."

The meeting still hadn't been called to order, and Mitko listened to several conversations at once, and many of them were simple introductions as leaders shook hands. It sounded like during his imprisonment the Coalition leaders had made a strong effort to persuade smaller countries from across Europe and Asia to join them. It was evident that many of the leaders were participating for the first time. The original Coalition had now expanded to become a miniature version of the United Nations.

A man at the head of the room pounded a gavel down on a podium several times, and the leaders took their assigned places. The room was organized in a semi-circle of desks ten rows deep so that everyone was facing the front of the room. The Russian leader went to the podium and stood before them. After a few welcoming remarks, he said, "I know most of you want to know what really happened to our army in America and how we could possibly have been defeated. So let's get that out of the way first."

The assembled leaders murmured their agreement, and the Russian continued, "We all know an invasion of America has been a dream of my countrymen for many decades. First we felt it would come through nuclear war, but then it became obvious that such an attack would destroy both countries. So we outlined a less destructive plan that would allow us to keep their cities and resources intact with little damage. This would allow us to repopulate the land with our own citizens. But we knew it would've been impossible to defeat the Americans when they were at full strength. First we had to let the United States weaken itself from within. We expected this to take several more years, but all of the pieces came together rapidly in the past decade.

"As the U.S. economy fell apart and civil unrest increased in their cities, some of our agents who were secretly stationed there approached key government officials who were already known to be opposed to capitalism. In fact, some of these officials had already implemented socialistic policies into their government. They listened eagerly as our agents outlined our plan for a united world government—the Coalition. All they had to do to be a part of it was look the other way as we moved forward with our invasion plans. To our delight, many of these American leaders went along with our plan and didn't alert their countrymen. Of course, it helped that we rewarded them handsomely. As you know, the loyalty of almost anyone can be bought for the right price, and these leaders fulfilled their part of the bargain."

One of the representatives raised his hand. "So these American leaders were on our side long before the invasion happened?"

The Russian shrugged. "I suppose it would be fair to say they were on both sides, and they planned on sticking with the group that came out on top. But yes, many of the highest American officials were secretly partners with us, with the agreement they would be given positions in this global government."

Another delegate called out, "I worked with the Americans, and they seemed completely devoted to their country. Give us an example of what you're talking about."

The Russian nodded. "The vast majority of the American leaders weren't aware of our plans, but we had just enough of them in our pockets to make it work. For example, when our battleships moved into position in the Atlantic and Pacific oceans, we should have never been able to get so close to their shores. Thankfully for us, those leaders purposely caused a lot of confusion and doubt about how America should respond. These distractions affected the decisions of the U.S. military advisors at crucial times, and their hesitation bought us just enough time to accomplish our goals. Otherwise our invasion never could have happened."

"Who were these American leaders that helped us?" another delegate asked, looking around the room. "Have they arrived here yet?"

The Russian waved his hand. "Their names don't matter now, and you can see we don't have any Americans among us. Frankly, they were fools to believe we'd ever include them in our group. If they could so easily betray their own country, how could we expect them to stay true to us? That's why we hit certain parts of Washington D.C. so hard at the beginning of the invasion. We knew where their offices were, so we eliminated them first—much to their surprise, I'm sure."

"But does anyone know the current military situation in America?" a dark-skinned man asked. "Even though the Coalition forces were somehow driven out, I believe with our combined strength we should be able to return and conquer anyone who is still there."

"That would seem logical," the Russian said. "However, we have among us a young man who participated in the invasion as part of our Coalition army. He was captured by the Americans and spent time there as a prisoner before escaping and making his way back to us. Let me introduce you to Mitko Petrov. He will share with us what he witnessed there."

Mitko didn't realize the Russian had even seen him enter the room, but he stood up and nervously walked to the podium under the scrutinizing stares of everyone in the room. He adjusted the podium's microphone and began by expressing how honored he felt to be among them, pacing himself so that the translators could keep up with him. Then he told his story exactly as he had during his previous appearance in front of the Coalition leaders, outlining how the American forces had outwitted them.

Mitko then said, "The sad truth is we threw away the opportunity of a lifetime. At the time of the invasion, never before had the United States been so divided, and the people were incredibly lax and unprepared. However, while our attack finished off the United States' government, we didn't destroy America. The Americans are now more powerful than ever. Our attack simply wiped away the corrupt government and got rid of the unproductive members of their society. In some ways, our attack greatly helped them. The people who remain there are strong and united. Their leaders have restructured their government into a central organization known as Zion, and it would be suicide on our part to send armies there right now. They are like a lion that has been roused from a long sleep and won't be caught off-guard again."

Mitko's comments were met with an uncomfortable silence. Many of the delegates had expected him to say how weak America was. The Russian arose from his chair and stood next to Mitko.

"I like this young one," the Russian said. "He speaks directly, and we need to abide by his wisdom to avoid another disaster. Just like Mitko, I feel we should wait on attacking America again until we have solidified other areas. As you know, several nations haven't joined with us yet. The British Isles and the Scandinavian countries have been particularly stubborn, and Israel has rejected any type of compromise with us."

The mention of Israel brought forth some restlessness from the leaders of the Muslim countries, who greatly desired to eliminate the Jewish people from the face of the earth.

The Russian held up his hands. "So let's focus our attention on these non-committed nations. They need to realize they really only have two options. In the coming weeks, we will convince them it is in their best interest to join us—or we will crush them into oblivion."

CHAPTER 6

Doug Dalton was driving one of the Springville group's supply trucks making its way south on Interstate 15 through Utah Valley. The supply trucks were a couple hours ahead of the bus convoy that was carrying the rest of the Saints who were returning to rebuild the city.

Doug's wife Becky sat next to him with their three children in the truck's back seat, and they were all quietly looking out the windows in wonderment at their former home. It was a crisp autumn day with a beautiful blue sky, but it was striking to see how brown and dead the landscape looked compared to the perpetually green grass of New Jerusalem.

"I never thought I'd be here again," Becky said, feeling a mixture of happiness and nervousness. "You're sure everything's all right in the city? There aren't some of our old neighbors still around who might try to kill us?"

"We'll be fine," Doug said. "The scout team has assured us that no one is living in Springville."

Becky sighed, hoping he was right. The past two weeks had been a bit crazy as they got organized for the return to Springville. There were about 350 people in their group, and a man named Stewart Schultz had been called as the bishop of the newly organized Springville First Ward. Bishop Schultz had once served in a Springville stake presidency and was thoroughly familiar with the city's layout and resources. Doug had known the new bishop for years, and he was thrilled with the choice.

The Springville group had met three times while they were still in New Jerusalem, and during the third meeting Bishop Schultz and his counselors had given callings to most of the ward members. Becky was called as the First Counselor in the Primary presidency, while Mark was asked to serve as the high priest group leader. Meanwhile, Michelle was called as the Nursery Leader, partly to help with Daniel. The bishop was aware of Doug's calling as one of the 144,000, and they both knew he'd be functioning in that capacity again soon, so he wasn't given a ward calling.

"Wow, look at that," Doug said as they took the north Springville exit and headed east over the overpass. "The mud from the flood almost completely covered the Maverick station and ruined the Flying J."

The Daltons had moved to the Jolley's Ranch camp before the flood from the Deer Creek and Jordanelle reservoirs had roared down Provo Canyon and devastated the lower portions of the valley. They had heard from Tad about the damage the flood had caused, but it was still shocking to see it with their own eyes. The citizens who had remained after the Saints had departed for the mountains had done their best to clean off the roadways, but some of the flooded buildings—such as the Maverick station—would never be usable again.

Since it was known that the floodwaters had damaged most of the homes west of Springville's Main Street, the group had agreed to meet at the chapel located on the corner of 300 East and Center Street. Most of the group had originally lived near the middle of town, so that building had a familiar feeling for them.

Mark and Michelle had also driven one of the trucks, and as they pulled into the church parking lot, Mark motioned to Doug to follow him. He rolled down his window and said, "I think we've got time to check out my house before the buses arrive."

The Daltons' home was only a block away from the church over on 100 North, and it was strange for Doug to pull into the driveway of his childhood home. They all got out of the trucks and walked through the house. Someone had rummaged through everything, and the family room reeked of bottled cherries from when Tad had lived there for a few days after the flood, but everything was certainly fixable.

"Dad, it really doesn't look too bad," Doug said. "You might be able to live here again."

"That's what I was thinking," Mark responded. "Maybe you could take the home next door. Remember how your house was filled with a two-foot layer of mud? I'll bet it's as hard as a rock now."

Doug nodded. "Yes, I think our house is out of the picture. Besides, if the Center Street building is going to be our main meetinghouse, I'd rather be close by."

"That's a good idea," Mark said.

Doug turned to his wife. "Becky, I know you wanted to start teaching at Sage Creek Elementary again, but that's out in the middle of nowhere now."

Becky nodded. "I know, but the old Grant Elementary building is just south of here and probably wasn't flooded too badly. I'll bet that could work out for us."

✦ ✦ ✦

Within an hour all of the buses had arrived, and everyone pitched in to get the luggage unloaded so the buses could start their trek back to New Jerusalem to pick up a group of Saints who would rebuild another city.

As the buses pulled back onto Center Street, the Daltons scanned the group for Bishop Schultz. He was usually easy to find by looking for his tuft of white hair.

"There he is," Doug said, pointing toward the meetinghouse steps. They approached the bishop and saw he was talking with a stocky, dark-haired man who looked familiar.

Doug approached the man and asked, "Jason Williams? Is that really you?"

The man turned and smiled. "Doug! It's great to see you! I suspected you'd be coming back here."

Jason was one of Doug's distant cousins, and they had even

lived in the same ward in the 1990s, but they hadn't seen each other for several years.

"Did you ever make it to New Jerusalem?" Doug asked. "I looked for you on the membership website a while ago, but your name didn't come up."

"Nope, I've been here in Utah as a maintenance missionary during everything that's been going on," Jason said.

"You must have seen some scary stuff," Becky said.

"Well, it's certainly been an adventure," Jason said with a shrug. "For a while I helped transport food to the missionaries in the outlying temples using a railroad system we patched together. Sherem's men would try to attack us, and we had to fend them off. Thankfully now that Sherem is dead, we don't need to worry about them anymore."

Bishop Schultz stepped toward them and said, "Jason is going to give the group a briefing on our situation here in the community, so please help me gather everyone around."

Bishop Schultz introduced Jason to the group, who then explained his role over the past couple of years as one of the 300 maintenance missionaries serving in the Salt Lake Valley. Jason said that after Sherem's death, the prophet had asked the missionaries to spread out from Idaho to central Utah and evaluate which cities were in the best shape in terms of repairable damage and electrical capability. That's how the prophet selected the cities he listed in his message to the Saints in New Jerusalem.

A woman raised her hand and asked, "Our home was on the west side of town. Will we be able to live there soon?"

Jason shook his head. "The homes on the west side of Main Street received extensive flood damage and we haven't even tried to get the power on there yet. Maybe by springtime. And as for those of you who had considered living in the mansions along the foothills, nearly every one of them has been severely damaged by the earthquakes. We had a couple of quakes hit last year that even sent some houses tumbling down the hillside. The homes up there just aren't safe."

"That brings up another point," Bishop Schultz said. "The missionaries have only restored the electricity to the central part of town, so we ask you—at least to begin with—to select a home within three blocks of this chapel."

Doug and Mark looked at each other, happy with that announcement, since Mark's home was easily within that range.

Jason spoke up. "Also, choose a home with a fireplace or a wood-burning stove. The natural gas lines coming from Wyoming were ruptured during the final round of earthquakes, and it will be a while before the lines are repaired. So the furnaces won't be operational until then. We'll be asking each household to help us cut and retrieve firewood over the next few weeks to create a stockpile for the winter."

"Thank you, Jason," Bishop Schultz said. "That's all for now. Obviously, if you have a home within three blocks, you have the first right to claim it. At first I was going to simply assign you a home, but let's begin by letting you select a home that best fits your needs. I'm going to turn you loose for a couple of hours, and if you find a home you like, write down the address and bring the information to me. We'll be making sandwiches for ourselves at six o'clock in the cultural hall. See you then."

Suddenly families were scattering in all directions and running down the streets as if they were on an Easter egg hunt. The bishop looked at Mark and shook his head. "Ahh, how easily we slip back into our materialistic ways," he said. "Hopefully there won't be too much bickering."

Mark smiled. He had stayed near the bishop so he could ask a question that had been on his mind.

"I was wondering how we'll handle property ownership," Mark said. "What if someone comes here in the spring and another family is now living in their old house?"

The bishop sighed and smiled at Mark. "That's a concern the General Authorities also had, but they feel that with the dissolution of the state and federal governments, all of the home titles and ownership documents are no longer valid. Of course, in your case as a member of the first group here, you naturally should be able to move into your previous home if you want."

"That's what I plan to do," Mark answered.

"The other unspoken factor in rebuilding the city is that this is a test of commitment for the Saints," Bishop Schultz said. "We both know there are some Springville families who stayed in New Jerusalem with the full intent to come here once winter is over—after we've done all of the hard work. That's fine, but should they have the right to kick someone out of their old home and move in when they get here?"

"I don't think so," Mark replied. "I feel if a family chose not to come with this first group, then they forfeit their claim to their house."

"The General Authorities agree with you," the bishop said. "There will be a Council of Fifty organized for this area that will enforce laws that pertain to such instances, but we're hoping that living the Law of Consecration for the past couple of years has taught the Saints how to get along and not focus so much on their possessions. I'm sure there'll be some cases where we'll be asked to work things out between the individual families, but we'll just see how it goes."

By that evening, each of the families had reported back on the home they had selected to live in, and Bishop Schultz was pleased with their choices. Nearly all of the families had chosen rather modest homes that were comfortable but not extravagant. A few of the families who had many children selected larger homes with several bedrooms, but that was understandable.

The day after the group's arrival in Springville, three 18-wheelers pulled up to the meetinghouse. The trailers were filled with a variety of foods, and these items became the basis of the Bishop's Storehouse. The next day Bishop Schultz and his counselors met with each family and gave them basic items to take home such as canned meat, flour, and sugar. The bishop explained that every once in a while there would be a ward dinner, but otherwise the families were expected to cook for themselves.

There had been some chilly nights, and everyone sensed winter could arrive at any time, so one of the top priorities was to help everyone make sure their homes were in good shape, such as repairing any broken windows. Some of the homes that weren't being lived in were excellent sources for replacement doors or windows. The Saints were doing a great job of making do with what they had available.

Doug and Becky looked at a couple other homes on the same block as his parents' house, but they finally decided to take Mark's suggestion and move next door to them. It was a nice red-brick home with a basement that gave them plenty of room. Becky really liked the large garden area in the backyard. She was also happy that the oven in their new home was working. It was an older model, so it had been overlooked by the people who had been stripping each home of what they thought was valuable.

Within two days they were settled in. While Becky was baking some bread, she heard a shout from Doug, who was clearing weeds from the garden area with Heather and Justin. She hurried out the back door and saw the three of them intently staring at something on the ground.

"Honey, come see this," Doug said as she came closer.

A creature about ten inches long squirmed near her feet, and she jumped back. "What is it?" she cried.

"It's a baby rattlesnake," Justin proudly told his mom.

Becky instinctively grabbed both of her children by the arms and pulled them back a few feet as Doug took a rake and steered the snake away from his family. It coiled up and snapped repeatedly at the rake.

"At first I thought it was a watersnake and I was about to pick it up, but then it snapped at me," Doug said as he grabbed a bucket and prodded the snake inside it.

"I hope there aren't any others around here," Becky said.

Doug shrugged. "I've never seen one this far into the city, but things have changed. I've heard some of the other families have encountered raccoons, deer, and even a bobcat. So nature has done its best to reclaim the city. We'll just have to be careful."

The next day Becky was sorting through a closet and came across a copy of the *Provo Daily Herald* that had an article on the front page with the headline "Thousands of Mormons Still Hiding in the Mountains."

The article was by a reporter who had tried to reach the Heber Valley Girls Camp, but he had been stopped by guards about a mile from the camp entrance. The rest of the article then slammed the LDS Church and criticized its leaders for causing such an unnecessary evacuation.

The final portion of the article read, "*State officials are trying to determine what to do when these extremist Mormons realize their folly and return from the mountains feeling hungry and disillusioned. The jobs they gave up will no longer be available, and their homes will have been foreclosed on and occupied by someone else. Fortunately, most Utah Mormons didn't heed their prophet's bizarre evacuation order and are doing well for themselves. Hopefully they'll be charitable toward their misguided friends when they wander back into the valleys.*"

"That's some really objective reporting," Becky said to herself. "Yep, we were the crazy ones."

She checked the newspaper's date and realized it had been published two weeks before the Coalition invasion. She shook her head, thinking of so many friends who had ignored the prophet's call and had shared the same attitude as the newspaper reporter.

She also found copies of *People* magazine and *TV Guide*. She looked at the dates on the covers, and they were also published just before the Coalition invasion. She flipped through them, and judging from the articles, a reader wouldn't have had any hint America was on the verge of collapsing.

The stories in the magazines featured the usual celebrity gossip about award shows and entertainment events. Becky had often read both magazines, but now she realized how shallow and trivial those things really had been.

"The beautiful people partied right to the end," she said sadly. "I wonder how many of them are even alive now."

She closed the magazines and folded up the newspaper, then took them into the front room where Doug had a small blaze going in the fireplace. She tossed them on the flames and watched as the pages burned, making the celebrities' perfect smiles crinkle and turn black before crumbling into the ashes below.

The group's first Sunday meetings together had some awkward moments, since most of the members were still casual acquaintances rather than lifelong friends, but these were minor annoyances compared to the stresses they had endured the past two years. Bishop Schultz turned Sacrament Meeting into a testimony meeting, and many people expressed how excited they were to be back in their hometown.

At the end of the meeting, the ward's executive secretary came up to Doug and said, "We've received a message from Elder Smith of the Quorum of the Twelve. He wants to meet with you tomorrow morning on Temple Square."

He handed Doug a printout of the message, which also said Doug should plan on being in Salt Lake for at least a week. The purpose was to bring together all of the members of the 144,000 living in the area and to organize the area's government.

Doug read the message to Becky, who said, "Don't worry, we'll be fine. Your parents and the neighbors will help me out."

The next day Doug stood with Elder Smith near the south wall of the Salt Lake Temple. Doug had been the first to arrive, and they were waiting for other members of the 144,000 to join them.

Doug looked up at the towering skyscrapers of the City Creek Center that loomed above them south of Temple Square. The Church had finished the construction on the project in 2011— seemingly just in time to abandon it.

Doug turned to the apostle and said, "I know you were involved in the decision-making process concerning the City Creek Center. At the time, it seemed like a foolish endeavor to some people. They figured we were heading to New Jerusalem, so what was the point? But I understand why the Church made such an effort. The complex is now ready for the Saints to occupy it."

"You're right," Elder Smith said. "Over the years, the Church had acquired vast amounts of money through their investments, and the Church leaders knew as well as anyone that the money would soon evaporate into thin air when the economy collapsed. President Hinckley was particularly concerned that these financial resources not be lost forever. So through inspiration and wisdom, he spearheaded several projects, such as completing the many girls camps that later served as refuges for the Saints. He also pushed forward the building of temples in areas he knew would become Cities of Light."

"It did seem that there was an accelerated pace on those projects," Doug said. "President Monson certainly kept up the momentum right until the nation began crumbling."

Elder Smith nodded. "The First Presidency worked closely with the Presiding Bishopric to determine other ways the money could be used, and that's how the City Creek Center came to be. Not only has it beautified the area, it also serves as the final piece to surround Temple Square with Church-owned buildings. And as you mentioned, the prophet knew that someday the Saints would return here, and now these buildings are available for our use both today and in the Millennium."

Elder Smith paused and chuckled a little. "I remember when one of the other apostles complained about the constant construction around Temple Square during one of our meetings. The prophet pointed a finger at him and said, 'I don't like the traffic delays and noise any more than you do. I realize we'll probably both be dead and gone by the time we're finished with this project, but someday the Saints will greatly appreciate what we've created for them.'"

"He was right," Doug said. "Now there's no need for more

construction here in the downtown area. Everything's in place."

Instinctively, Doug reached out to touch the wall of the temple. The granite felt solid and cool against his hand. There was something special about the Salt Lake Temple that symbolized the entire history of the Church.

Elder Smith watched him and smiled. "It's good to be back, isn't it?"

Doug nodded happily. "I love New Jerusalem, but this is home."

Within a half hour, Elder Smith and Doug were joined by several other men who had been serving as members of the 144,000 high priests. Doug recognized a few of them from the day they were initially given their callings in Denver, and he was eager to hear their stories. Everyone listened closely as one man told of his experiences in southern California.

"I had served my mission in Long Beach, so after we were called that's the first place I went. I was amazed at the destruction all along the shoreline. I suppose part of it came from the Coalition invasion, but most of it was caused by natural disasters. I saw a lot of evidence of severe earthquakes, and at least one major tsunami. There was tons of seaweed plastered against the western side of the buildings and there was other debris piled everywhere, including a sailboat upside down in a yard nearly a mile inland."

"Wow, that kind of wave probably finished off anyone who was still living there," Doug said.

The man grimaced slightly. "I did see a lot of bodies, but it was like the entire shoreline had been scoured clean. So I headed west and eventually reached the Redlands Temple. I was thrilled to find 300 Saints living there, and they were happy to hear that New Jerusalem was going to be built. I stayed with them for a few days, then they started on their journey to Zion. When I finally returned to New Jerusalem I tracked them down and was glad to see they had settled in well."

A few more stories were told, then Elder Smith said, "Let's go into the temple and begin our meeting. We have a lot of material to discuss."

During the meeting, Elder Smith explained the purpose of the Council of Fifty, and how it was a separate governing organization from the Church's leadership tier. Bishops and stake presidents weren't invited to be on the council, but members of the 144,000 could be if needed, since they weren't ecclesiastical authorities.

Each of the repopulated cities throughout Utah and Idaho had a representative on the Council of Fifty, and they formed the equivalent of a state legislature. Doug was assigned to serve as a member of the council as Springville's representative, and his main responsibility would be to supervise the city's citizens as they elected a mayor and city council. Several other members of the 144,000 were also called as their city's representative, with the understanding that this should be a temporary position until the cities were firmly established and a suitable replacement could be found.

Toward the close of the meeting one of the men said, "I thought I saw electric lights on the hill as I was coming into the valley this morning. Were my eyes deceiving me?"

"No, we do have electricity restored to parts of the city," Elder Smith said. "A few hundred Saints from Idaho were asked to resettle Salt Lake soon after Sherem's death, and they moved into the area north of here known as The Avenues. They've done a good job getting their basic utilities working, and they've even restored phone service to their homes. So based on their success, I think we'll be able to have each of your cities prospering within a short time."

CHAPTER 7

The repopulated cities throughout Utah and Idaho did indeed flourish, and as late November approached, the prophet encouraged the Saints throughout America to celebrate Thanksgiving Day on the traditional fourth Thursday of the month. The Saints knew they had much to be thankful for during the past few months, particularly for the dedication of the New Jerusalem Temple and the return of the Ten Tribes.

Almost as soon as New Jerusalem had been established, various farms had been started on the outskirts of the city to raise cattle, pigs, and turkeys, and these farms were now producing abundantly. As a special treat to the Saints, the leaders of the Church made sure frozen turkeys were transported to all of the cities of Zion, allowing each family to have a turkey dinner on Thanksgiving.

As December arrived, the weather remained mild. It had only snowed once in Utah, which helped the Saints make great progress in rebuilding the cities along the Wasatch Front. Then as Christmas Day approached, a snowstorm left a couple of inches on the valley floor, helping create a holiday spirit.

The Christmas season now had a different feel compared to the commercialized holiday that had developed prior to the Coalition invasion. The Saints emphasized that the Savior wasn't really born on December 25th, but rather in the springtime when the shepherds of Bethlehem would be in the fields tending their flocks.

However, the Church leaders felt they shouldn't overlook an opportunity to celebrate the Savior's life, so the First Presidency sent a message asking the Saints to gather on the grounds of a temple in their area on Christmas Day, where several uplifting activities were planned.

The Saints in Springville were invited to travel to the Payson Temple. Becky and her children Heather and Justin had been invited to participate in a play that focused on the Savior's life. Scenes were enacted from his mortal life, including his birth and ministry, and then his crucifixion and resurrection in Jerusalem.

Then the play moved forward to the depiction of Jesus' visit to the Nephites and the Ten Tribes, followed by the appearance of Heavenly Father and Jesus to young Joseph Smith in the Sacred Grove. The play concluded with an enactment of the Savior's Second Coming. It was done in a simple manner, but the Spirit was strongly felt, because the Saints knew the time was very close for the Savior's return, when they hoped to see the marks in his hands and feet for themselves.

On that day in Jerusalem, Josh had awakened feeling a bit depressed. He knew his family and friends would be celebrating the Savior's life that day, but as he looked across the city, it seemed like any other day.

Josh shook his head. He was standing in the city where the most important event in the history of the world had taken place— the Savior's suffering for the sins of the world—yet the people in the city below didn't realize their Messiah had already come. Just as importantly, they didn't realize he was coming again soon.

He awakened Colton and said, "Merry Christmas."

Colton sat up in bed and looked around the room. "Where are all the presents?"

Josh smiled. "Sorry, Santa Claus didn't bring us anything this year. But I was thinking we could give ourselves a gift we'll never forget."

"What do you have in mind?"

"Let's go spend some time in the Garden of Gethsemane."

Colton nodded. "That's an excellent idea."

By mid-morning the apostles stood at the foot of the Mount of Olives, looking at the quiet grove known as the Garden of Gethsemane. The grove was now within the walled grounds of the Church of All Nations, and as they entered the grove, they were able to look back at the eastern wall of Jerusalem.

"Not much has changed in 2,000 years, has it?" Colton said. "I imagine the Savior and his disciples looked across this valley just like we're doing."

The garden was empty, and the apostles agreed to go to separate areas of the garden and contemplate the Savior's life for an hour or so. As special witnesses of Christ, they had both received a personal visit from him soon after their callings as apostles, but they sensed this visit to the garden would give them a needed boost of spiritual strength.

Josh moved to a far corner of the garden and sat down against an ancient olive tree. He had brought along his scriptures, and he opened his Bible and read the chapters in the Four Gospels that told of the Savior's final days, including his suffering in that very garden.

He wept openly as scenes from those dark hours prior to the crucifixion passed through his mind. He could visualize the events as if he were actually there, and he thanked the Lord for granting him the privilege of witnessing them.

Finally, he turned to Doctrine and Covenants 19:16-19 and read, "*For behold, I, God, have suffered these things for all, that they might not suffer if they would repent;*

"*But if they would not repent they must suffer even as I;*

"*Which suffering caused myself, even God, the greatest of all, to tremble because of pain, and to bleed at every pore, and to suffer both body and spirit—and would that I might not drink the bitter cup, and shrink—*

"*Nevertheless, glory be to the Father, and I partook and finished my preparations unto the children of men.*"

Josh closed the scriptures and gave a prayer of thanks for the privilege of serving as one the Savior's apostles. He looked across the garden at Colton, who was deep in prayer. After a few minutes, Colton stood up and the apostles walked toward each other.

Colton grasped Josh's hand. "Thank you for suggesting we come here. I've been deeply blessed and strengthened."

"I have too."

The apostles then slowly walked from the garden, feeling better prepared to face the challenges that would soon be coming upon them.

CHAPTER 8

As the new year began at the Kremlin, Mitko Petrov was becoming increasingly integrated into the Coalition membership. For whatever reason, the Russian leader had really developed a fondness for him, saying Mitko reminded him of himself when he was young. Mitko wasn't sure whether this was a compliment, but he could live with it if it kept him safe.

The whole scenario was a curious situation, but Mitko likened himself to the Old Testament prophet Daniel, who found himself in a foreign country as a servant to a powerful leader. The only real moment of conflict Mitko had faced was when the Russian gave him a bottle of wine as a gift, but Mitko quickly said alcohol caused him severe stomach pain. The Russian just shrugged and drank the wine himself.

Mitko was glad the arrival of the representatives from smaller countries had tempered the warlike attitudes of the original Coalition leaders. The overall plan still included global conquest, but at least now there were productive discussions about how to accomplish it, rather than rushing headlong into another battle.

Then one day brought a startling turn of events. The Syrian representative requested that a special guest be allowed to address the group that afternoon. The request was granted, and as the leaders were settling into their seats for the meeting, there was suddenly a commotion at the back of the room. Everyone grew quiet as the Syrian led his guest toward the podium. The guest confidently walked to the front of the room and cordially greeted each of the main Coalition leaders, bowing slightly to each of them. Mitko instantly recognized the man's olive skin, green eyes, long black hair, and flowing robe.

"What is Elias doing here?" he asked himself.

Mitko had been serving his mission in Nebraska when Elias was doing a speaking tour at universities across the United States, and Mitko remembered having intense discussions with members of the Church about him. Several members that Mitko visited with had believed everything Elias said. "His prophecies are always on the mark," they would tell him, but it still didn't feel right.

Josh Brown was serving as the stake president in that area, and Mitko and his companion went to talk to him about Elias. President Brown had told them, "I know he's not a prophet, but he has the personality and talents to either bless or destroy the lives of many people. I'm just not sure which way things will go."

Mitko glanced at the charismatic figure standing a few feet away and thought to himself, "It looks like I'm finally going to get the answer."

Elias conferred briefly with the Syrian representative, who then motioned Elias toward the podium. Elias adjusted the microphone then held out his arms and said, "I am Elias of Syria, and I come to you as a brother and a friend. I'm grateful these esteemed leaders have granted me a few minutes of your time to share what I have learned. I recently spent a few weeks in Jerusalem conversing with the Jewish leaders in an effort to determine their true intentions."

This news certainly caught everyone's attention. The fate of Israel was always a hot topic among the Coalition leaders.

"For the most part, the Jews are a unified people," Elias said. "They're confident that their God will protect them, and I think we all agree that they've had an amazing streak of luck over the past few decades. There's no logical explanation for Israel's survival, and yet they continue to prosper."

His comments produced shouts of agreement from the other leaders. Israel had always been like a sliver under their collective fingernails—always festering, and sometimes causing more irritation than it ever should have.

"I don't tell you this to arouse anger against the Jews. I suppose we could leave Israel alone for some time and they would continue to isolate themselves. I have been told that the British Isles are your next intended target, and I see the wisdom in that move. I truly don't have a personal interest in your war games, but before you make a final decision about your next target, you should be aware of two men who have recently arrived in Jerusalem. I sense that they could not only be a threat to the security of my home country, but possibly even to the Coalition's global plans."

Elias wanted to make himself clear. "I have met thousands of people throughout the world, but these two men possessed a strength—a tangible power—that I had never felt so strongly before. They told me they were apostles of the LDS Church, Elder Brown and Elder Negus. Their presence in Israel concerns me. Why are these Christians teaming up with the Jews?"

Mitko felt the blood drain out of his face. Josh Brown was in Jerusalem!

Elias then paused for a full fifteen seconds before saying, "I propose that eliminating these apostles should be a top priority before their influence grows—even if that requires destroying Israel in the process."

There was immediately some murmuring among the leaders. The representative from Saudi Arabia raised his hand. "I thought you sought only peace and harmony. Are you seriously asking us to attack Israel?"

Elias smiled. "I'm only the messenger, seeking you to help keep my own country safe from destruction. If Israel grows stronger, that obviously poses a direct threat to Syria. I am indeed a peace-loving man, but I see how the elimination of Israel and these apostles would actually bring sustained peace to the world. I'm certain that after a damaging attack, any Israeli survivors would be humbled enough to finally join the Coalition." He paused before adding, "There are times when force is required to create peace."

These comments were first met with silence, but then a smattering of applause grew into a steady roar. The Russian and

Iranian leaders were seated side by side, and they smiled and nodded at each other. The Iranian leaned over and whispered to his friend, "If we can shift the blame for attacking Israel onto Elias, then what are we waiting for?"

CHAPTER 9

Following Elias' stirring comments, the Coalition leaders ended the meeting and moved outside to a large courtyard for dinner and to personally meet Elias. The unusually warm, clear day was welcomed after a long cold spell, and the leaders basked in the sunshine. Elias stood under a canopy and graciously greeted each of the leaders for nearly two hours before excusing himself to rest in an apartment that had been provided for him.

Mitko had filled a plate with food and had taken a table close to the canopy, pretending not to listen to the conversations. As the leaders talked, it was clear that Elias' idea to attack Israel was well-received. Such talk made Mitko feel sick to his stomach, and although he really wanted to ask Elias about the apostles, he felt restrained by the Spirit to even hint he had an interest in them.

A few minutes after Elias had departed, Mitko noticed the sky turning a strange bluish color to the east. At first glance it appeared as if a large dark cloud was approaching, but the cloud seemed to dance and jolt back and forth in the sky.

Mitko looked around to see if anyone else had noticed it, but they were all too wrapped up in their food, liquor and conversations to focus on anything else. Mitko felt the hair on his head stand on end. Something was definitely not right.

"*Go to your room now and block any openings,*" a voice told him. He had heard this voice before, and knew the Spirit was guiding him. He quietly slipped out of the courtyard and went to the small one-bedroom apartment he had been given in a large building about a block away. The bedroom had one small window, and he taped some plastic over it. Then he crammed a blanket into the crack under the apartment door before locking it and pushing his desk in front of it. Finally he climbed into his bed, pulled up the blankets and waited anxiously for something to happen.

Within moments a buzzing sound could be heard outside the building. Suddenly hundreds of black objects forcefully pelted the window. Mitko climbed out of his bed long enough to see that the objects were actually large horseflies, frantically seeking to get into the room. He climbed back under his blankets as screams of terror filled the building.

Someone banged on his door and violently shook the handle. A man shrieked, "If anyone is inside, let me in! They won't stop biting me!"

Mitko stayed motionless as the man finally gave up and ran down the hall. Mitko tried not to imagine what was happening in the courtyard, but the continued screams of terror said more than enough.

The monstrous swarm of horseflies attacked the citizens of Moscow for more than an hour before moving on to the west, blocking the sunset as they flew away. Mitko felt prompted to stay in his room until morning as the shouts of pain and anguish continued throughout the night.

In the morning he felt he needed to make an appearance, so he bundled himself up in a blanket, covering himself as much as possible. He knew he likely was one of the few who hadn't received bites, and he didn't want to be asked why he'd been spared.

He went down into his building's lobby expecting turmoil, but he wasn't prepared for the scene before him. Hundreds of people were lying on the lobby floor, all of them with horrible bite marks on their faces, necks, and arms. Many of the wounds were already filled with pus and clearly infected.

Mitko couldn't see any doctors or nurses in the room. It was as if these people had been abandoned to their fate. He felt compassion for them, but he couldn't see how he would be of any help, so he quietly walked toward the exit. Several people called out to him, moaning in misery, but he moved out into the street and headed toward the Russian leader's residence.

When the housekeeper cracked open the door to the leader's luxurious apartment, Mitko could tell things were not going well. First of all, the housekeeper herself had several bandages on her face to cover the sores that had developed.

"Come in," she said quietly. "Seeing you will hopefully raise his spirits."

Mitko was ushered into the Russian's bedroom, and he tried not to gasp. The leader's head was one large oozing sore, and his eyes were nearly swollen shut. Some of the sores had already developed tiny maggots from eggs laid by the flies.

"Oh, Mitko, I hope you were spared the worst of the attack," the Russian said.

"I was, thankfully. I'm so sorry that you weren't," Mitko said. He knew the Russian was an evil man, but the leader's current condition made it almost impossible to not feel some sympathy for him.

"The swarm was upon us so quickly," the Russian said weakly. "I dived under the table, but they just kept attacking me."

He let out a moan, then lay back on his bed in agony. One of the Russian's aides asked Mitko about the condition of other people in the Kremlin.

"It's very bad out there," Mitko told the aide. "The lobby of my apartment building is filled with injured people, and in every building I passed I heard dozens of people crying out in pain."

Mitko stayed in the leader's apartment throughout the day, listening as reports began coming in from most of the other Coalition nations. There were apparently several massive swarms crossing Asia, rather than just one. The swarms had first appeared in Japan and China, and then they had worked their way west, with the European nations and those near the Mediterranean Sea expecting to be targeted in the following days.

"I can't imagine this," the aide said as she hurried off to get more gauze to rewrap the leader's sores. "I've never heard of such an occurrence."

Mitko simply nodded as she went into the next room, but he had studied the prophecies enough to know this wasn't some strange fluke of nature. A similar incident had happened in Old Testament times to the Egyptians who had threatened the Children of Israel. Plus, he had been aware of the signs of the times since his days as a missionary and had been watching for the seven plagues that would be poured out upon mankind before the Second Coming. He quoted Revelation 16:1-2 in his head.

"And I heard a great voice out of the temple saying to the seven angels, Go your ways, and pour out the vials of the wrath of God upon the earth.

"And the first went, and poured out his vial upon the earth; and there fell a noisome and grievous sore upon the men which had the mark of the beast, and upon them which worshipped the image."

He looked over at the Russian leader and said quietly, "If this doesn't qualify as the first of the seven plagues, it's awfully close."

By the next day, people were beginning to die from their sores and the unknown disease the horseflies had transmitted to them. Mitko was asked to join the ranks of healthy men who were collecting the bodies and burying them. It was a horrible task that he expected could go on for days, but he still felt the Lord's hand in his current situation. Perhaps he was only there to serve as a witness to the effects of the plague among the wicked.

"Heavenly Father, please let me carry on," he prayed. "I only seek to do thy will."

CHAPTER 10

That same morning, Josh Brown could hardly believe the sight before him as he looked out the window of the BYU Jerusalem Center. The rising sun was being blocked by what appeared to be a dark cloud dancing in the sky.

"Colton, come here," Josh said. "You've got to see this."

His fellow apostle was soon by his side, and they watched in shock as a giant swarm of horseflies descended on the city. Within seconds they were filling the city below and soon they were pelting their window. A few flies managed to get into the room through a small gap in the window sill and they flew right at the apostles.

"Stuff something in that window!" Colton shouted as he picked up a book and took a swing at one of the flies.

Josh hurried to the window with a wad of paper towels, which he crammed into the opening and blocked any additional flies from entering the room,

Colton found a fly swatter on top of the refrigerator and began to do battle with a dozen flies, while Josh did his best with a broom.

"Ouch!" Josh cried out, clutching his neck. "One bit me!"

Within seconds he had received two more bites, but Colton's quick reflexes with the flyswatter soon had eliminated all of the flies. He used the swatter to lift a fly off the floor to look at it more closely. It was the largest fly he had ever seen, and the piercing mouth parts were unusually large.

"These beasts are brutal," Colton said.

"Tell me about it," Josh said, clearly in pain as he examined a bite on his arm. It appeared as if the fly had actually tore through the skin. It was bleeding, as were his other bites.

"Please give me a blessing," Josh asked Colton. "I hate to think what diseases these things are carrying."

"I would be glad to," Colton responded. He put down the fly swatter and placed his hands on Josh's head.

"Joshua Brown, by the power of the holy Melchizedek Priesthood which I hold, I command you to be healed of the wounds you have just received and that your body will be made whole. This will be done according to your faith, so that you can move forward with your mission here on earth. I do this in the name of our Savior Jesus Christ, Amen."

The apostles opened their eyes, and to their slight astonishment the wound on Josh's arm began to shrink. Within seconds the injury was completely gone. Colton had seen many miracles in his lifetime, but even he was a bit surprised at how quickly the healing had occurred.

Josh reached up to the bite on his neck, and it had disappeared as well. He then humbly knelt down and thanked Heavenly Father for healing him.

"Thank you for that blessing," Josh told Colton. "I already feel so much better."

They swept up the flies they had killed and put them in the trash, then they returned to the window and watched helplessly as the flies continued their assault on Jerusalem. A previous occupant had left a pair of binoculars in a drawer, and Colton focused in on one of the major streets in the city. People were running in a panic, and if someone fell down or even stopped, dozens of flies were instantly upon them. Colton finally couldn't watch anymore, handing the binoculars to Josh.

"What do you think is causing this?" he asked. "These flies seem like ferocious super-mutations. It just seems so strange for them to come during the winter. Shouldn't the cold weather have killed them off?"

"We've had such a mild winter that it must not have affected them," Josh replied. "Besides, I feel they are sent by the Lord."

"Really? What in the world makes you think that?"

Josh grabbed his scriptures from the table and opened them to Doctrine and Covenants 29:17-20. He read, *"And it shall come to pass, because of the wickedness of the world, that I will take vengeance upon the wicked, for they will not repent; for the cup of mine indignation is full; for behold, my blood shall not cleanse them if they hear me not.*

"Wherefore, I the Lord God will send forth flies upon the face of the earth, which shall take hold of the inhabitants thereof, and shall eat their flesh, and shall cause maggots to come in upon them;

"And their tongues shall be stayed that they shall not utter against me; and their flesh shall fall from off their bones, and their eyes from their sockets;

"And it shall come to pass that the beasts of the forest and the fowls of the air shall devour them up."

Colton shook his head. "That's awful. I hope you're wrong, but what we're seeing could certainly be the start of that."

✤ ✤ ✤

The apostles each had two suitcases of clothes on the plane when they had departed New Jerusalem, but their suitcases had been destroyed when John's plane crashed. Since that time they'd been wearing the clothes they had parachuted in, plus a couple of suits that Benjamin Cohen had provided them, but they definitely needed more clothes. So that evening Colton searched through several other dorm rooms and found some white shirts and tan pants that would fit them. He brought the clothes back to their room and showed them to Josh.

"The prophet asked all of the apostles to wear light-colored clothing in public, and I feel we should do our best to still follow that counsel here in Jerusalem," Colton said. "Besides, it will help the people identify us as we go among them."

"That's a good idea," Josh said. "We'll make do with what we have. I'm glad you found these clothes."

By the next morning, the swarm of flies had mostly departed, but there were still some buzzing around. It had been a long night for the apostles. They couldn't stand to be cooped up any longer, knowing that people were suffering in the city, and they felt a need to see how Benjamin Cohen was doing.

They were eager to assess the situation in the city, but before they left the building Josh offered a fervent prayer to the Lord that they would be protected from the remaining flies. Then they began walking toward the heart of the city. Many flies circled around the apostles, buzzing right in their ears, but to their relief they weren't bitten.

Soon they stood on Benjamin's doorstep. They knocked loudly, and although they could hear people talking inside, no one would answer the door. Finally they went to one of the windows, where a woman was looking out at them.

"We need to speak to Benjamin Cohen," Josh said to her through the glass. "Can you tell him we're here?"

The woman shook her head. "He's very hurt and is sleeping right now."

"Was he bitten by the flies?" Josh asked her.

"Yes, it was terrible."

"We could come in and give him a blessing of comfort."

"Comfort?" she asked with a shake of the head. "Some people think that you two are the cause of the flies."

The apostles looked at each other in surprise. "Us? We're here to bless the people, not hurt them."

"I don't know. We were safe while Elias was here. Now that he has left and you have arrived, this terrible plague has come upon us. Is that just a coincidence?"

The apostles sensed they weren't going to change the feelings of this superstitious woman, and they finally waved good-bye.

"Tell Benjamin we'll return later," Josh told her before walking with Colton across the street to a vacant lot where many young children had gathered to suffer together. All of the children had been severely attacked by the flies and were lying on the ground in misery. Josh looked into the eyes of an Israeli girl who had bites all over her face. "Where are your parents?" he asked her.

"They've left us here to go take care of themselves," she said.

"That doesn't seem fair," he told her. "I want to help you. Do you believe in God?"

"I do."

"Do you believe that God can heal you from these bites?"

"Yes. But how?"

Josh put his hands on her head and said in a loud voice, "In the name of Jesus Christ and by the power of the Melchizedek Priesthood, I command you to be healed!"

Then he stepped back, and the other children gathered around. To the girl's great joy, the bites and sores began to close up. Within thirty seconds her skin was smooth and free of blemishes.

"Thank you so much," she said joyfully, showing her healed arms to her friends. "Can you heal my friends too?"

"Yes, through the power of God."

Colton joined Josh in blessing the children, and through the power of the priesthood the apostles healed everyone in the vacant lot. The children rushed down the street, shouting that they had been healed, and the word quickly spread.

Soon there was a mob scene as people rushed toward the apostles, but Josh stood on an abandoned car and told the crowd to form two lines in order to receive a blessing. The crowd did so, and each person would come forward and kneel before one of the apostles, and then go away rejoicing as their bites vanished. It was an amazing display of priesthood power, and Josh's heart filled with emotion as he pictured the Savior performing similar healings long ago in this same city.

An hour later, the woman who had been at the window of Benjamin's home across the street was now at the head of the line in front of Josh. He was surprised to see her.

"Hello again," he said, remembering how cold she had been toward him earlier.

She looked a bit embarrassed. "Mr. Cohen has awakened and

has heard about the healings you're doing. He wants you to visit him. I'm sorry about what I told you earlier. He doesn't believe you caused the flies. That was my own belief, but now I know I was wrong."

Josh nodded. "Thank you. Tell him we'll come as soon as we can break away from the crowd."

For the next two hours, the apostles continued to heal people until finally Josh motioned for Colton to move toward Benjamin's home. As they reached the door, they promised to come back outside in a few minutes. The woman was waiting for them and rushed them into a room where Benjamin was sitting in a chair near the window.

"I've been watching you," he told them. "I've never seen anything like it in my life. You truly possess the power of God."

Colton nodded. "That's the whole reason we're here—to help you and your people fulfill the promises made by the prophets."

Benjamin smiled. "Then would it be all right if you gave me a blessing as well? I feel miserable."

The apostles both moved forward and placed their hands on his head, and as Josh pronounced the blessing, Benjamin was healed. He held out his hands, watching the sores go away.

"What a miracle," he said gratefully. "Please bless the members of my household as well."

The apostles did so, and then they noticed the crowd outside the house had grown larger.

"We need to get back out there before a riot starts," Josh told Colton. The apostles told Benjamin they would be in touch with him soon, and then they moved back outside into the crowd. The blessings continued throughout the day, and the people just kept coming. As the apostles' strength began to falter, the woman from Benjamin's house brought them sandwiches and water, and they thanked her profusely. As nightfall approached, Josh finally announced to the crowd they would have to stop for the day but would return the following morning.

✠ ✠ ✠

Shortly after nightfall, the apostles returned to the Jerusalem Center, physically exhausted but exhilarated by what had transpired that day.

There was soon a knock on their apartment door. They looked at each other in surprise. "It can only be one person," Colton said, moving toward the door. He opened it to see John the Beloved standing there holding several sets of light-colored clothing, including a white suit for each of them.

"You've been very busy," John said. "The Lord is pleased with your efforts. Plus, I've brought you gifts. Sorry your clothes went up in flames."

"Thank you," Josh said, taking the clothes from him and hanging them in a closet. "I'm just grateful to hold the priesthood and be able to heal these people. We'll be back at it tomorrow."

"That's good," John said. "It's difficult to see people suffering like this, but through these healings, the people are developing a personal connection to you, and they'll be receptive as you teach them the full gospel plan in the coming months."

"That's how I feel," Josh said. "We are careful to emphasize that they are being healed by the power of God, rather than having them worship us."

"That's the right way to do it," John replied.

"So is that the end of the fly swarm?" Colton asked. "Are the flies going to reach America?"

"No, they've all nearly died out. They're still working their way toward the Atlantic Ocean, but that's as far as they'll go."

"If I may ask, is this the first plague you described in the Book of Revelation?" Colton asked. "It sure sounds like it."

"It is," John said. "As the scriptures state, this first plague mainly affected those who are fighting against the Kingdom of God."

"Kind of like a warning shot to the wicked?" Josh asked.

"I suppose, although it was more like a direct hit. The flies did a lot of damage, particularly among the people in the Coalition countries. But the plagues that follow this one will affect the whole world, even the Saints in America."

"How is Mitko Petrov doing?" Josh asked. "Did he survive this plague?"

"Yes, he followed the Spirit's promptings and was protected against the flies. He's living among the Coalition leaders and he's fulfilling his mission well."

"That's good to hear," Josh said. "I don't envy him, though. That's a challenging assignment. He's so young, yet he's been through so much already."

"That sounds a lot like you two," John said. "The main reason I'm here is the Savior asked me to give each of you a priesthood blessing of strength, comfort and confidence. It's easy to get worn down in such circumstances."

The apostles each received a beautiful blessing from John, and he specifically mentioned that their priesthood powers would be magnified in unexpected ways. As John concluded the blessings, he shook hands with them and said, "Stay strong, my brethren. No matter what happens, remember that angels are watching over you."

Then he vanished before their eyes.

CHAPTER 11

Doug Dalton had spent the day at a meeting with the Council of Fifty in Salt Lake, and as he pulled into his driveway, he saw a truck already parked there that wasn't one of the original vehicles the Springville group had driven. He saw Becky standing on the lawn talking to a man with a shaved head and a short goatee.

"Jonas Ferguson!" Doug said as he climbed out of the truck.

"I just thought I'd stop by," Jonas said with a smile.

Doug approached them and quickly gave Becky a kiss. Then he reached out to shake Jonas' hand. "It's great to see you, but what brings you here?"

"Well, I've never lived in Springville, but after your group left, all winter I felt I needed to join you," Jonas replied. "Becky said you could introduce me to the bishop, and hopefully I can get settled in."

"Sounds good to me," Doug said. "We can use your help getting everything rolling this spring."

Jonas smiled. "That's what I hope to do—get things rolling. As you know, I've been working in the New Jerusalem vehicle recycling center, and we've basically got Missouri and Kansas all cleaned up. I figured you might need someone to get a recycling center going here as well. What do you think?"

"Absolutely. As I drove back from Salt Lake today, I probably passed a thousand abandoned cars. I'm sure we can get you a good crew. That will be a great project that will really improve things around here."

"That's great!" Jonas said. "I can't wait to get started."

That night Doug quickly fell into an exhausted sleep, but Becky had a hard time dozing off. Something didn't feel quite right. She finally got up to check the house, and as she passed Daniel's room he cried out in pain. This surprised her, since he rarely made any noise, much less cry. She went to his side and found he was gasping for breath. She picked him up and rushed him into their bedroom.

"Doug! Wake up! Daniel's in trouble."

Doug sat up and looked at his son. Daniel was turning blue and was twisting and turning in agony.

"I need to give him a blessing," Doug said, motioning for Becky to sit with Daniel on the edge of the bed. Doug then stood next to her and laid his hands on his son's head.

"Daniel Dalton, by the power of the Melchizedek Priesthood, I bless you that . . . I bless you that . . ."

Several seconds of silence passed as Doug looked down at Becky with tears in his eyes. Then he continued with the blessing he was being prompted by the Spirit to give.

"Daniel, you can go to your heavenly home now. I bless you that your release from this mortal body will be without pain. You may join your relatives who have passed on and are waiting for you in Paradise. Your mission on earth is complete. You have served valiantly, and the Lord has other work for you to do in the Spirit World. In the name of Jesus Christ, Amen."

Daniel looked up at his father and took two more labored breaths. Then he was gone. Becky clutched her son tightly and began to sob, hardly believing what had just happened.

"I'm sorry," Doug told her, his heart breaking. "I just couldn't bless him to be healed. The Lord wanted him to return home."

Doug contacted Bishop Schultz first thing in the morning about arranging for someone to dig Daniel's grave.

"We want to hold a short graveside service for Daniel," Doug told him. "I have several relatives buried in the Evergreen Cemetery, and I'm hoping he could be buried next to his great-grandpa Jack. I think there's an open space next to him. I can go dig the grave myself if needed."

"Don't worry, we'll take care of it," Bishop Schultz said. "I actually talked to Jason Williams a couple of weeks ago about the cemetery, and he's had some families helping get it cleaned up. So it should be in good shape."

Later that morning Jonas knocked on the Daltons' door. He had heard about Daniel's death and was struggling with his emotions. When Doug answered the door, Jonas burst into tears as the two men held each other for a few moments.

"I don't know if you really understand how important Daniel was to me," Jonas finally said. "When I went to Manti, I had every intention of making sure all of you died at the hands of Sherem's men, but Daniel changed my heart. Would it be all right if I built a coffin for him?"

"We'd be honored," Doug said.

Jonas began by searching through some of the unoccupied homes until he found a set of nice wooden cupboards that he could adapt for the coffin. He removed the cupboards from the wall and then carefully pieced the small coffin together, even making sure the hinges worked properly. Finally he found some sandpaper in a garage and smoothed the entire surface, inside and out.

"You deserve so much better than this, little Daniel, but I did my best for you," Jonas said to himself as he looked at the finished coffin.

Early the next morning he took it to the Daltons, and Becky teared up when she saw it. "It's beautiful," she said, giving Jonas a quick hug. "Thank you so much."

Doug laid a nice blanket in the bottom of the coffin and then gently placed Daniel's body inside it. Daniel's siblings Justin and

Heather each took a moment to say good-bye to their brother before Doug gently closed the lid.

They met Bishop Schultz at the cemetery, as well as Doug's parents, who had traveled there early that morning to show Jason where to dig the grave next to Grandpa Jack. A few other ward members had also come, and the Daltons were appreciative of their support.

Doug and Jonas carefully placed the coffin next to the grave that Jason had dug, and Becky and the kids stood in front of it. Doug then invited everyone else to gather around.

"Thank you, Jason, for your hard work this morning, and also thanks to everyone for your support at this time. Daniel was such a special boy, and he made a great impact on all of our lives."

Doug got a little choked up, but he cleared his throat and continued, "Daniel faced physical challenges even before he was born. When the Coalition attacked, Daniel was inside Becky's stomach. The chemicals that were released when the Coalition tanks destroyed the Dugway Proving Grounds blew over us when we were in Spanish Fork Canyon, and I feel that's the reason he had some physical ailments. But we believe our mortal bodies will someday be resurrected and emerge perfect and whole. I can't wait for the day when Daniel will rise from this grave and wrap both of his arms around me."

Jason had been standing quietly nearby. He hadn't planned to take part in the service, but he knew he should share an experience he had witnessed. He stepped forward and quietly asked Doug, "Could I speak for a few moments?"

Doug nodded and motioned for him to stand before the group. Jason gave a nervous smile and said, "I just wanted to tell you about something I saw last year while I was serving as a maintenance missionary in Salt Lake. This was before Sherem's death, and I always had to be cautious to avoid being caught by his men. I soon found the safest place for me to sleep was in the Salt Lake City Cemetery, since Sherem's men were afraid to go there after dark. I usually slept under a tree on the slope where several of the presidents of the Church were buried. It was usually silent there, but one night I was awakened by voices coming from up on the slope. Two men in white robes were standing in front of the headstone of one of the prophets. They were happily talking to each other and one of them even glanced down the hill in my direction."

Jason paused, holding back his emotions. The group was silent, eager to hear the rest of the story.

"I just stayed motionless and watched them," Jason continued. "One of the men recited a prayer that sounded similar to a healing blessing, and then suddenly that beloved prophet emerged from the ground. He was dressed in white, looking young and happy. Then he stood in front of his wife's grave and recited the same prayer, and soon she was standing next to him!"

Doug was definitely intrigued by Jason's story. "Did the ground literally open up?"

"No. I suppose a resurrected body can just pass through the coffin and the soil. Anyway, then the four of them went to another prophet's grave and repeated the process for that prophet and his wife. Then they all vanished and I was left alone. After a few minutes I walked over to the graves where this had happened. Their headstones were still in place and the ground looked undisturbed. The amazing thing to me is that it felt completely natural and right. Well, I'm sorry I interrupted the service, but I can testify that some people are already being resurrected, and we'll all have that privilege someday."

"Thank you for sharing that experience," Doug said. "That's wonderful."

Bishop Schultz suddenly remembered something else he could add to Jason's account.

"I don't know if you've heard this," Bishop Schultz said, "but all of the modern prophets appeared on the stand at the dedication of the New Jerusalem Temple. I saw them with my own eyes, and I can remember wondering if they had been resurrected, because they sure looked solid to me. Since Jason's experience happened the summer before the temple dedication, I feel confident the prophets were resurrected beings when I saw them in the temple."

"That makes sense," Doug said. "Brigham Young had said the Lord would resurrect Joseph Smith as soon as his mission was complete in the Spirit World, and I'm sure that applies to the other modern prophets as well."

Doug then concluded the service by dedicating the grave by the power of the priesthood, asking that the site would be watched over and protected until the resurrection. Then he stepped away, and the group watched silently as Jason and Jonas carefully placed the coffin into the grave.

The men shoveled several scoops of soil onto the coffin and then invited others to assist them. Justin stepped forward and although it took some effort because of his small stature, he placed several scoops into his little brother's grave before handing the shovel back to Jason.

"Daniel was so kind to me," Justin said. "Although we couldn't talk to each other, we knew what each other was feeling. I'm going to miss him so much!"

✦ ✦ ✦

Daniel's spirit hovered in the air unseen by his family and friends at the graveside. He watched as the grave was filled, and his heart was touched as he heard his brother's words.

"Thank you, Justin, for always watching out for me," Daniel said. "Now I'll do the same for you."

Daniel smiled at the many ancestors who were accompanying him. He was once again a full-grown spirit, clothed in heavenly glory, and the past several hours had been marvelous as he had become reacquainted with his extended family in the Spirit World. He was eager to begin some assignments he had already been given to help prepare the world for the Second Coming, but he paused for a moment to reflect on what he had learned during his three years inside that deformed mortal body. As one of the most valiant of Heavenly Father's spirit children, he had been given the opportunity to come to earth in a situation that would serve as a teaching moment for him and also for his family as they learned humility in dealing with his physical challenges.

One aspect he had enjoyed in that body was that the veil had remained very thin for him. He had always been aware of his key earthly assignment—to evoke a sense of compassion in Jonas on that crucial night in Manti—and he was grateful he had been able to fulfill it.

Jason and Jonas had put the finishing touches on the grave, and now Doug and Becky stood next to it with their arms around each other. Daniel glided close to the ground and put his arms around his parents. He knew that someday his spirit would enter that body again—except then it would be a perfect resurrected body—and he would be raised by Doug and Becky during the Millennium.

"I'll see you both soon," Daniel told his parents before rejoining his ancestors who were still watching nearby. His Grandpa Brown clasped his arm and said, "Are you ready?"

"Yes, let's get to work!" Daniel replied, and they quickly slipped back through the veil into the Spirit World.

CHAPTER 12

It was a somber February day for the Daltons as they pondered life without Daniel, but by afternoon Doug knew his son wouldn't want him moping around. Doug had been meaning to talk to Jason Williams about some of the conditions in the valley so he could move forward with his calling, and he figured it was a good time to do that. He tracked Jason down at the meetinghouse, where he was replacing a broken window.

"I wanted to thank you for everything you did for us today," Doug began. "I know it wasn't easy to dig the grave on such a chilly morning. We couldn't have done it without you, and I really appreciated the experience you shared with us. I know it helped all of us realize the resurrection isn't far away."

"You're welcome," Jason said. "It was the least I could do."

Doug looked up at the broken window. "I know you're busy, but do you have a few minutes to talk?"

"Sure. I think this window can wait."

Doug nodded gratefully. "As you know, I've been asked to supervise the missionary work in this area, and I'm hoping you can tell me what it was really like here in the valley after we went into the mountains. For example, how many of the Church members survived who didn't go to the camps?"

"Well, not many," Jason said. He pointed west toward Lincoln Point, the community that was built on the shores of Utah Lake at the base of West Mountain. "The kids out there are really the only ones that survived, and if Utah Lake wasn't so full of trash fish for them to eat, they would have died too."

"What happened to all of the adults?" Doug asked.

"Well, after the invasion, Sherem and his gang of criminals controlled everything north of Thanksgiving Point, and the flood had wiped out most of the low-lying areas from Orem to Spanish Fork. So a lot of families headed south right after the flood, but a gang of thugs was controlling travel on I-15 past Santaquin."

"So where did they go?" Doug asked.

"At first, many of them moved into homes near the Payson Temple, but it was strange for me to see these people cluster around the temple like that. These were the same people who had ignored the words of the prophet when he told them to gather to the mountain camps."

"I guess these people recognized they hadn't done what they should have—a little too late," Doug said. "I wish they would've just come to the camps. We were very cautious about who we let in, but if they were sincere, we would've given them a second chance."

"I think it was a matter of pride," Jason said. "They couldn't admit they were wrong, but these people had no clue how to live without a well-stocked grocery store down the street. That's when some families went to live in Lincoln Point, where they at least could catch fish to survive."

"That's not much of a life," Doug said.

"Exactly, especially after having nice homes and cars, all kinds of techno gadgets and plenty of food. I spied on the city a few weeks after the families moved there, and it wasn't pretty. The kids were blaming their parents for the situation they were in. They had actually divided into two groups—the adults versus the children. Soon their anger boiled over into bloodshed, and it wasn't long before there weren't any adults left."

"That's terrible," Doug said. "So do you think these kids are beyond hope in terms of the gospel?"

Jason frowned. "I don't know. Most of them were raised in LDS homes and had a spark of light in them at one point. Are you thinking of sending missionaries to visit them?"

"Yes, but I realize it won't be an easy assignment. I've got two people in mind who should be able to handle the task, though. How about the tag team of Jonas Ferguson and Mighty Tom?"

Jason grinned. "You mean the new guy with the goatee and that big red-haired kid that lives in the Provo Temple? That just might work!"

Two days later Doug stood in the parking lot of the Center Street meetinghouse with Jonas and Tom. They had just finished filling the back of a truck with an assortment of fruits and vegetables and covered it all with a tarp.

"I expect our peace offering will be accepted," Doug told them. "We'll win over their stomachs first, then go from there."

Before they departed, Doug took the opportunity to give each of them a blessing of protection and guidance. Then the pair climbed into the truck and headed west, with Jonas behind the wheel. They got on 400 South and crossed the overpass near Wal-Mart, which gave them a good view of their destination. The smoke from several bonfires rose from the city and filled the western sky.

Jonas' mind drifted back to the last time he was in Lincoln Point. It had been the day after Tad North had escaped from him, and Jonas had been angry enough that if he'd found Tad that day he would have likely killed him. He shuddered to think how much worse his life would have been if that had happened.

As they approached West Mountain, Tom pointed to the side of the road. "We've been spotted," he said. "There's a band of kids running back to the city."

Jonas was a little concerned. "What should we do?"

"I say we just keep going," Tom said. "I'm not too worried. I don't think they have a real leader."

Within minutes they entered the city, and on both sides of the street were teenagers making threatening gestures. It was mostly the boys that were being aggressive, while the girls stood back in small clusters, unsure what was going on. They all wore raggedy clothes and looked like they hadn't bathed in months. They all had long hair, and it was hard to tell the boys from the girls, except for the boys' scruffy beards. Also, a few of the girls held babies in their arms, and others were clearly expecting soon.

Jonas pulled the truck in front of the city hall, where Tom hopped out and climbed onto the side of the truck. He called out, "Hello, we come in peace, and we've brought food for all of you."

The kids looked at each other in surprise, not sure to believe him, but then Tom pulled the tarp away so they could see the food.

Suddenly a boy called out, "Hey, Tom, is that you?"

Tom peered down into the crowd and recognized one of his former classmates from junior high.

"Darren! How are you doing? I didn't know you were here. Come help us pass out this food."

The rest of the group seemed shocked that one of their own people actually knew Tom, and they quietly watched as Darren went forward and grabbed a bag of apples from the truck. Several other kids instantly crowded around him like a pack of animals.

"Hey, don't push each other," Tom said. "There's enough food for everyone."

Jonas had joined him on the side of the truck, and they began handing out bags of apples, pears, and carrots. Soon each of the kids were eagerly munching away.

"I hope a little nutrition isn't too much of a shock to their systems," Jonas said half-jokingly.

Tom tried to count how many kids were gathered around the truck, and he estimated there were less than 200 of them. He got down from the truck so he could talk to Darren a little more privately. Jonas stayed in the back of the truck and kept handing out food. The kids' appetites seemed insatiable.

"Is this everyone?" Tom asked Darren. "Didn't there used to be a lot more of you?'

Darren nodded. "At one time there were about a thousand of us, but that terrible winter really wiped us out."

"I'm sorry to hear that," Tom said. "I know you've been through some very hard times. The main reason we're here is to help you. If some of you want to stay here, that's fine, but we'd love to have you come back to Springville. We'd help you all get back to a normal life."

Darren's eyes gleamed. "You'd really do that for us?"

"Absolutely."

"Why don't you ask everyone?" Darren said excitedly.

"I guess that would be best," Tom said. He climbed back into the truck bed, which was now half-empty.

"I think they were hungry," Jonas said, handing out more apples.

"That's good," Tom said. "It should help our cause."

Tom stepped on the side of the truck again and let out a whistle, capturing everyone's attention.

"I've been talking to Darren, and he thinks some of you might be interested in moving to Springville. The people there would provide you with food and a nice home, but they'd expect you to help out as we rebuild the city. That would be better than living here, wouldn't it?"

Most of the kids nodded, but one girl shouted, "But aren't they all adults? They'll just make us follow their rules."

Tom nodded. "Yes, there are both adults and kids in the city, but they're all very kind. If you decide you don't like it there, you can return here."

A boy called out, "I grew up in Payson. Could I live there instead?"

"There are settlements being established in Springville, Spanish Fork and Payson. You would be welcome to live in any of those cities."

Another girl said, "But aren't they all Mormons? What if I don't want to be one?"

Jonas stepped up and said, "No one will make you become a Mormon. I wasn't a Mormon until a couple of years ago, but I love it! I think you would, too."

The group grew silent, and Tom said, "Well, I think we're nearly ready to go. Raise your hand if you want to stay here and not go with us."

About twenty of the boys raised their hands. "Thanks for being honest with us," Tom told them. "You'll have this town to yourselves. But if you change your mind, just come find us."

One of the boys yelled, "We'll be fine on our own."

"I'm glad to hear it," Tom said. "So please give those bags of apples to someone else."

Tom's comment surprised them, since they each held a bag of food. They hesitated before tossing the apples toward some of the girls and marching away as a pack into the city hall.

Once they were out of the way, Tom said, "Let's get moving while we still have plenty of sunlight. Jonas, take some of the young moms and their babies and go tell Brother Dalton and Bishop Schultz we're on the way. I'll start walking with the group to Springville. See if they can send some extra trucks."

Jonas helped several expectant mothers into the back of the truck, then he drove to Springville. He soon pulled up to the Center Street meetinghouse and rushed inside. He found Doug talking with Bishop Schultz.

"What happened?" Doug said, concerned. "I didn't expect to see you for a few days."

"Tom already convinced most of them to come live with us," Jonas said. "He's leading them here right now."

"You're serious?" the bishop asked.

Jonas grinned. "Yep, you're about to add 200 Young Single Adults to the ward."

Bishop Schultz rolled his eyes. "Can you imagine what those interviews are going to be like?"

The three of them quickly got coordinated. The bishop contacted several Relief Society sisters to come help with the girls, while Doug found another supply truck he could drive to help pick up the remaining young mothers and their children. Meanwhile, Jonas loaded several containers of water into his truck that he could take to the group.

By sundown, several round-trips in the trucks had been made, and the Relief Society had already taken the girls into their homes by the time Tom and the boys made their way up Center Street. Doug and the bishop stood in the middle of the road, eager to welcome them. Tom was grinning widely, enjoying the moment. In some ways he felt like a chief leading his warriors home.

Over the next couple of days, each of the kids who had come from Lincoln Point were given new clothes, haircuts, and plenty of food. A good number of the young people decided to live in Payson or Spanish Fork, where they had lived before, leaving the Springville Saints with about 70 individuals to integrate into their community. Bishop Schultz and Doug did sit down and talk with each of them, and the men were pleased to see that nearly all of the kids had been humbled by their experiences. They promised to keep the laws of the city and were just happy to have a sense of normalcy back into their lives.

The kids also indicated that they weren't actually the ones who rebelled against the adults. In fact, they survived mainly because they hadn't taken part in the conflict. Many of their original leaders were either killed or suffered major injuries that later took their lives during the brutal winter that followed.

As Bishop Schultz told Doug, "One boy told me he had felt like a coward to hide during the battle, but now he's just grateful to be alive."

Tom stayed in Springville for a couple of days, but then he told Doug he was going to return to the Provo Temple. "I'll stay in touch with you," he said. "I haven't forgotten about those 20 guys still living out there. We'll let them live on their own for a while, but I plan on paying them a visit in a couple weeks to see if they've changed their minds."

Doug smiled. "That sounds good. Let me know when you want to go. I'm sure Jonas would like to go with you."

One of the youngest girls who had left Lincoln Point was named Tara, and Doug and Becky had taken her into their home. She got along well with their daughter Heather, and for the first couple of days the Daltons let her just rest and regain her strength. Then at the dinner table after Doug gave a blessing on the food, Tara suddenly blurted out, "I'm a Mormon, you know."

"I'm glad to hear that," Doug said. "Do you remember very much about going to church?"

"I do, and I had good parents." She paused, on the verge of tears. "I had just started to go to Young Women. I think I was called a Bee's Nest. Does that make sense?"

Becky smiled at her. "Yes. The 12 and 13 year old girls are called Beehives."

"Yeah, that was it. But I was just feeling confused about everything. My parents kept talking about going to live in the mountains, and it scared me. I was happy with how things were. So on the day we were supposed to go to the mountains, I packed up some clothes and went to my friend's house. They weren't going to the mountains, and she had said I could hide in her bedroom. So that's what I did."

"Did your parents ever find out what happened to you?" Doug asked her.

"Nope. But after a couple of days my friend's parents found out I was there, and they kicked me out. They said they were afraid they might get accused of kidnapping me or something. So I just wandered the streets for a few weeks. It was horrible."

"Then how did you end up at Lincoln Point?" Becky asked.

Tara shrugged. "People on the streets kept telling me that Lincoln Point was where all the fun was, so I eventually made my way there. What a mistake!"

Tara paused again for a few moments to wipe her eyes. It was clear she had gone through some horrible experiences there. The Daltons were quiet, letting her work through her emotions. Finally she said, "I can remember my parents saying something about a place called New Jerusalem. They planned on helping build it someday. Do you know if it exists?"

The Daltons all started talking at once. Doug quieted the others down and said, "We certainly do. That's where we've been living before we came here. It's a beautiful city."

Tara's eyes sparkled. "Really? Is it far away? Maybe my parents are there!"

"Yes, it's pretty far," Doug said, "but if your parents are there, we have ways to find them, if that's what you want."

"Oh yes, I really do."

Doug smiled at her. "My sister Emma lives there, and I'm sure she would love to help you find your parents."

"That's wonderful," Tara said through tears. "I miss them so much."

Becky spoke up. "Doug, your parents had talked about going back to Zion to pick up some computer equipment for the church buildings here. Maybe they could take Tara to Emma's house."

"I know they'd love to help you," Doug said. "We'll go talk to them right after dinner."

CHAPTER 13

---❖---

Three days later, Mark Dalton stopped his truck in front of his daughter Emma's home in New Jerusalem.

"We're here," Mark said to his wife Michelle and their passenger Tara. It was a modest brick home, but they couldn't help notice the lush green lawn and vibrant flower beds that were planted along the house.

"It's only March, yet look how beautiful and colorful everything already is here," Michelle said, pointing to a clear-blue pond across the street filled with geese and ducks.

Tara looked back at the city center with its spectacular buildings, including the incomparable temple complex. "It's more wonderful than I could have ever dreamed," she said. "I really can't believe I'm here."

As they climbed out of the truck, the home's front door opened and Emma met them on the lawn. Her brother Doug had e-mailed her the day before that their parents were traveling to Zion, and he told Emma about Tara, along with the names of Tara's parents so Emma could start searching for them.

Emma gave her parents each a hug, then she turned to Tara. "I was excited to hear your story, and I think I've identified your parents here in Zion! I just want you to look at their photo to make sure."

Within moments they were gathered around Emma's computer as she opened up ZOOM, the Zion Official Online Membership website that contained a database of everyone who was a citizen of New Jerusalem.

"You looked for a Mike and Samantha Francom, right?" Tara asked anxiously, watching the screen.

"Yep, they should show up any second," Emma replied. The computer took a few more seconds to upload the page Emma had bookmarked, but then their names and an address appeared, along with a photo of a smiling couple.

"It's them!" Tara cried. "That's amazing!"

"It looks like they live just a couple miles from here," Emma told her. "Do you want to call them?"

Tara shook her head. "Let's just go see them!"

Emma and her parents could hardly keep up as Tara ran back to the truck, and a few minutes later they stopped in front of a small, well-manicured home. As Mark turned off the truck, Tara started to panic.

"What if they won't accept me back?" Tara asked. "I've done so many bad things."

"If they turn you away, you can come live with us," she said. "But I'm quite sure that won't happen."

Emma saw the curtains move in one of the home's windows, and a woman briefly peered out.

"Somebody's home," Emma said. "Let's say hello."

Emma took Tara's hand and led her to the door. Emma knocked gently, and a pleasant-looking blonde woman soon greeted them.

"Hello! Are you Samantha?" Emma asked.

"Yes, how may I . . ." she said, but she stopped as Tara rushed forward and embraced her.

"I don't understand," Samantha said, looking at Emma.

"This is your daughter," Emma said softly.

Tara let out a sob. "Mom, I've missed you so much!"

Samantha's eyes grew wide, and she grabbed Tara's shoulders and looked in her eyes. "Tara! Oh my goodness, it's really you! You've gotten so much taller!"

They embraced again, and soon a man came up behind them. "What's all the commotion?" he asked.

"I'm home, Daddy," Tara said, and the man looked dumbstruck, unable to fully believe what he was seeing.

"Mike, our prayers have been answered," Samantha said.

Mike joined his wife and daughter in an emotional group hug. After a few moments, Tara backed away and said, "I've hoped you both can forgive me. I was so awful to you before I ran away, and I've made some terrible mistakes since then. I don't feel worthy to be called your daughter. Emma said I can live with her if you don't want me."

Mike hastily waved his hand. "Tara, don't talk that way. We love you and can barely express how happy we are to see you again. This is a dream come true!"

Mark and Michelle joined them in their living room for a few minutes as Tara explained to her parents what had happened to her the past couple of years. Tara was an only child, and Emma could only begin to imagine the pain Mike and Samantha must've endured every day since Tara disappeared from their lives. But that anguish was ebbing away as they chatted with Tara. The prodigal daughter had miraculously returned.

When Emma and her parents returned home, they were in for a surprise of their own. First of all, Tad was already home, which was unusual during the day. He smiled at Emma and said, "I just wanted to let you know that the missionaries serving among the Ten Tribes will be honorably released next week, so David will be returning home soon!"

"Finally!" she said.

David's mission had been a curious challenge for Emma. The initial call had come as a surprise, and he was suddenly gone without really giving her time to mentally prepare for his departure. Then, unlike the previous generation's two-year calls, this one had been open-ended. At first the Church leaders expected the missionaries to be there for a few weeks, but then their time among the Ten Tribes had stretched on for several months. Emma was happy David was serving, but although it had been only six months, the unusual circumstances had made David's absence feel much longer than that, especially to his mother.

David's younger brother Charles spoke up. "I hope that means David can help me on my new assignment."

"What will you be doing?" Michelle asked. "We haven't heard about it."

Charles smiled at his grandma. "I've been asked to be part of a large youth group that will be helping with the landscaping in the valley of Adam-ondi-Ahman. We'll be clearing shrubbery, widening trails, pruning trees, and anything else that needs to be done in preparation for the big meeting that will be held there."

Mark looked at Tad in surprise. "Has there actually been an announcement about that meeting?"

"I haven't heard anything official," Tad said. "But the fact the Church leaders are making such a concentrated effort makes me think it can't be too far off."

Tad then turned to Charles. "So while I think David would like to be a part of the group, I'm guessing his decision will be based on what Phyllis is planning to do. I'll bet there are still some chemistry between them, even though they've been apart."

"Don't worry, I've already thought of that," Charles said. "I talked to Phyllis a couple of days ago and invited her to help us. When I told her David would probably be helping me, she was eager to join the group."

Tad shook his head and chuckled at his son. "Is this service project about landscaping or matchmaking?"

Charles smiled. "A little of both."

A week later, David eagerly pushed his face against the window of the train as it pulled into New Jerusalem's main terminal, watching for his family. He and several hundred other missionaries had been released the day before from their service among the newly settled Ten Tribes on the southern outskirts of the city. The prophet wanted them home by April 6th in time to celebrate Restoration

Day with their families. Since establishing New Jerusalem, the Church leaders had emphasized the importance of the day the Church was restored by Joseph Smith in 1830, and a variety of uplifting festivities were planned throughout that day.

That date had an added significance to many families in Zion, since it marked the second anniversary of when the Elders of Israel departed their homes to battle the Coalition forces. David's experiences as part of the army had boosted his self-confidence and helped him form an unshakable bond with his father.

David had thoroughly enjoyed every minute of his mission. He had particularly liked teaching the people from their own scriptures, *The Record of the Ten Tribes*. The missionaries had also taught from the other Standard Works, but nothing could compare to watching a family realize that the Savior had visited their own ancestors many years ago. The people had been warm and loving to them, and they had eagerly grasped the basic principles and ordinances of the gospel.

His father's generation of missionaries had talked about finding one or two golden families during their missions, but David and his companions had taught entire extended families nearly every week. He had grown so close to the Spirit, and he would've happily served longer, but so many of the young men among the Ten Tribes had already become elders in the Melchizedek Priesthood that they could now carry on the work among their family and friends.

David looked out the window again, and he could see the buildings on the BYU-Zion campus. He was eager to get back to his studies there and to find out how Phyllis was doing. She had written him a few times, but her messages certainly hadn't been romantic. He had received messages from his brother Charles during his mission saying Phyllis had been dating other guys, but he also knew not to trust his prankster brother too much. He was hoping he was still at the top of Phyllis' priority list.

As the train pulled to a stop, he could see his parents standing off to one side, with Charles and Leah in front of them. It was great to see them again, and as he stepped off the train, they hugged him tightly. He smiled at Leah and said, "You're turning into a beautiful young woman."

"Thank you," Leah said, happy to have her oldest brother back. "It will be nice to have you around again."

"I appreciate that," he said. "Hopefully Charles feels the same way."

Charles gave a sly grin. "I really intended to say something sarcastic, but actually, I'm very happy to have my old roommate back."

They all started walking toward the city bus that would take them home, and David couldn't help looking around a little. He'd really hoped that Phyllis would be there. His family was chuckling about something, and Charles nudged his brother with his elbow. "You seem to be looking for something."

"Ah, it's nothing," David replied, failing to notice that a woman wearing big sunglasses and a funny hat had been keeping pace with them a few feet away. Emma finally said, "Son, go try your missionary approach on that woman over there."

David looked over at the woman, and her smile gave her away. He walked over to her, pulled off the sunglasses, and looked into Phyllis' mischievous eyes.

"Why sir, are you a member of the Lost Ten Tribes?" she asked playfully.

David grinned. "Nope, but I'm happy to report they're not lost anymore. They've returned—and so have I."

"That's great news!" she said, barely containing her laughter.

David paused for a moment, then he said, "Oh what the heck," and gave Phyllis a bear hug that lifted her off the ground.

His family was laughing as they gathered around them, but Tad told his son, "That's all for now, Elder North, until you're officially released."

Phyllis stepped away with a smile, but as they continued walking toward the bus, she briefly linked arms with him and sent a tingle down his spine by whispering, "It's great to have you back."

❧ ❧ ❧

David and Phyllis spent all of Restoration Day together, holding hands as they walked through the exhibits on display on the plaza surrounding the New Jerusalem Temple. For Phyllis, it gave her a chance as a fairly recent convert to learn more about Church history than she had known before. They stopped at an exhibit about the Liberty Jail where Joseph Smith had been held prisoner for many months. Phyllis had never heard the full story before, and it moved her to tears.

"That's terrible how they treated Joseph," she said. "He sure sacrificed many things for the Church."

Then they saw an exhibit explaining the missionary efforts of the early apostles in England in the mid-1800s, and how thousands of those Saints later came to the United States and helped strengthen the Church.

"That's how my mom's side of the family joined the Church," David told Phyllis. "They came from England."

"Really?" Phyllis said in surprise. "I guess I just figured your family had lived in Utah for hundreds of years."

David laughed. "It probably seems that way, but the Daltons didn't leave England until 1865 when they came across the Plains and settled in Utah."

Phyllis gave him a coy look and asked, "Does that mean my children will have some English blood in their veins?"

Her comment left David momentarily speechless, but Phyllis merely laughed and gave his hand a squeeze before pulling him toward the next exhibit.

CHAPTER 14

In a different part of New Jerusalem, Kim Brown looked at a framed photo of her husband Josh that was next to her bed. She wiped away some tears, surprised at how much she was struggling with his absence this time. Part of the difficulty was that she hadn't been able to speak with him since the day he left.

She'd felt some anxiety when Josh was gone helping the Lost Ten Tribes travel to Zion, but that assignment was straightforward and she had always felt assured he would return safely. She wasn't so confident this time.

Kim had received a call from the prophet's secretary two days after Josh departed to let her know the two apostles had arrived safely in Jerusalem, but she hadn't heard anything since. She did her best to act calm and collected when she was attending her Church meetings, because the true nature and location of Josh's current assignment wasn't yet public knowledge. The First Presidency felt it would be best to let Josh and Colton get settled and begin their duties in Jerusalem before making any announcements to the Saints.

Of course, Elder Negus' wife Cindy knew all of the details, and they had actually met for lunch a couple times to discuss their shared burden. They were honored that their husbands were worthy and capable of such an assignment, but it made their hearts ache to realize they might not see their husbands for quite a while.

Kim looked once more at her husband's photo before climbing into bed and turning off the light.

"I love you, Josh," she said softly as she closed her eyes.

As she lay there, she thought back on a call she had received from Emma North a few days earlier, letting her know that their nephew Daniel Dalton had passed away in Utah. In some ways, Emma's message wasn't a shock to her, since Daniel had lived longer than many people thought possible. However, the news of his death affected her deeply, because it brought back memories of her sister Tina's death several years earlier.

To get her mind onto other topics, Kim finally got out of bed and checked her e-mail account. She was thrilled to see a message from her parents, Frank and Miriam Marlar, who had been serving as Church missionaries in Peru's mountain villages since before the Coalition invasion. It had been a couple of months since she'd last heard from them, and the timing of their message really lifted her spirits.

Her parents' mission call had originally been for 18 months in the Lima Peru Temple, but after all of the troubles began in the United States, they didn't have a safe way back home, so they just continued to serve in Peru. Miriam was of Peruvian descent and had many family members there, and they experienced tremendous success in sharing the gospel with her relatives and many others.

Kim's father Frank was particularly enjoying his time in Peru. He had come a long way from being the grouchy U.S. Air Force pilot Kim had grown up with as a father. Frank had been raised in the Church, but he had strayed from the right path in his late teens and had actually become antagonistic against it.

Frank's heart only got more hardened after the unexpected death of his daughter Tina in an auto-pedestrian accident. However—with lots of help from both sides of the veil—he had eventually become active in the Church again in his 40s. Now Frank was known to thousands of Saints throughout the Peruvian mountains as the "abuelo blanco" —"white grandpa"—who could convert entire families with his bold testimony of how the atonement of Jesus Christ had changed his life.

✣ ✣ ✣

Kim eagerly opened up the e-mail and began reading through it. It was written by her mother and read:

My dearest daughter Kim,

Thank you for your last message about Josh being sent away once again. You carry a heavy burden as the wife of an apostle, but we know you'll be blessed for your sacrifices.

Your father and I just came down from the mountains to the temple complex for the first time in several weeks, and so this is my first opportunity to contact you. We are still having a wonderful time. Your father is loving it here, and to be honest, we might never leave. This now feels like home to us.

I do have a special message for you today. Last Sunday as I was taking a quiet walk through a grove of trees, I felt someone walking alongside me. I turned and saw your sister Tina as clear as day. It nearly gave me a heart attack, but she smiled at me and told me she was staying very busy in the Spirit World.

In fact, she told me that even though your father and I have helped thousands of people join the Church over the past few years, she has been teaching even more people than that in the Spirit World. You and I did a lot of temple work already for our ancestors, but apparently there are thousands more there who were never recorded in my family's old records. Tina says these people have accepted the Savior's plan and are ready for their temple work to be done. She says she has a plan to get the information to us.

As we talked, we agreed that she should contact you, since you have access to all of those temples in New Jerusalem where the work could be processed and completed much more quickly.

So I am just giving you a heads up that your sister might suddenly show up soon. We love you so much, and hopefully someday we'll get to give our beautiful twin grandchildren a big hug!

Love, Mom

Tears came to Kim's eyes as she finished reading the message. She quickly sent a reply to Miriam that she had received the e-mail and that she would let her know when Tina visited her. Her heart burned, knowing everything in her mother's message was true. After all, Kim had actually seen Tina in the Spirit World when she had briefly died during an accident in Guatemala.

Kim read her mother's message again, then knelt down and prayed, "Dear Heavenly Father, please let me be worthy and prepared to visit with Tina. I'm eager to help my ancestors receive their temple ordinances. Plus, it would help me focus on something besides Josh's safety."

She closed her prayer, then said, "Okay, Tina, I'm ready whenever you are."

Kim put the twins to sleep, then rested quietly on her bed in the darkness. She listened intently to every sound, fully expecting Tina to appear at any moment, but nearly an hour passed. Then as she was about to doze off, she felt her spirit leave her body. She floated toward the ceiling and could see her body reclining on the bed.

"I'm dead!" she thought to herself. "Somebody help me!"

Suddenly a dazzling glow entered the room. Inside the glow was her sister Tina, easily identified by her long dark hair and brilliant smile. The sisters embraced, and then Kim nervously looked back at her body on the bed.

"Your body will be all right for a little while," Tina said. "I have something I need to show you."

"What about the twins?" she asked.

"You have friends here who will watch over your home."

Kim was surprised to see several angels were now in the room. They smiled at her and waved as Tina put an arm around Kim's waist and the sisters elevated through the ceiling. They flew through the air, passing above the brilliantly lighted New Jerusalem Temple. They continued to climb so that Kim could see New Jerusalem stretching for miles in every direction.

"The city is so beautiful," Kim said.

"It is," Tina responded, "but it's nothing quite like where I've been living. Hold on!"

Kim heard a "pop" and within a second they had left the nighttime of the mortal world and were in the perpetual sunshine of the Spirit World. Kim looked down at dozens of sparkling communities, all perfectly aligned. Large temples and other magnificent buildings were at the center of each city.

"Welcome to Paradise," Tina said happily.

Kim expected Tina to take her to one of the cities, but they kept flying along and soon passed over what appeared to be a great gulf of water.

"Where are we going?" Kim asked.

"I wish we could stop in Paradise and have you visit with some of our relatives, but we need to get to Spirit Prison," Tina said. "You can only be away from your body for so long."

They approached the gulf's shoreline and were soon passing over cities again. These communities were still beautiful, but they didn't match the ones Kim had just seen in Paradise.

"I'm guessing we're now in Spirit Prison," Kim said. "I can tell a difference."

"Yes, but this is still a nice area. Most of the people in these cities have accepted the Savior and are simply waiting for their temple work to be done. It gets worse the farther you are from Paradise."

Tina pointed toward a cluster of buildings that looked like a university. "There's our first stop," she said.

They glided to the ground in the middle of a large plaza and then entered a building. Tina waved to a woman who was monitoring the door, and she motioned for them to enter. The sisters soon stood at the doorway of a large room. It had a high ceiling and held about 100 chairs arranged like the "stadium seating" Kim had seen in some of the theaters on earth. The chairs faced a well-lit podium at the far end of the room. Almost all of the seats were filled, and the people were eagerly listening to an energetic young man teach them about the life of Joseph Smith. The instructor paused when they entered the room, and he clapped his hands with joy.

"I want to welcome a special visitor to our class," the man told the group. "Say hello to my Aunt Kim, wife of the apostle Josh Brown."

The class members turned and welcomed her with smiles and waves. Kim raised her eyebrows. "Daniel? Is that you?"

Daniel laughed. "I know I'm a lot taller now, but yes, it's me!"

He raced up the stairs to give her a big hug. "Thank you so much for everything you did for me on earth," he said. "I'm very happy you'll be assisting with our family's temple work."

"That's the plan," Kim said. "Tina's going to tell me more about it, I hope."

"Absolutely," Tina said. "Well, we need to be on our way, but I couldn't pass up the chance for you to see each other."

"It's been great to see you," Daniel told Kim as he gave her a final hug. "Tell my parents I'm very happy here. This is where I'm supposed to be."

The sisters were soon back in the air and traveling toward a towering peak in the distance. "That's our destination," Tina said. "Our ancestors live at the base of the mountain."

They settled onto a pathway built along the foothills of the great mountain. The nearby buildings reminded Kim of ancient Inca temples she had seen in books and documentaries, except these buildings sparkled like new.

Tina guided Kim down the path toward a large amphitheater built into the side of the mountain. It was completely filled with people.

"These are our relatives," Tina said. "There are more than 30,000 people here, and they're all waiting for their temple work to be done so they can enter Paradise."

A man in a white robe was speaking to the group on a large

platform as the sisters entered the ampitheater. He turned and smiled at them. "Our guests of honor have arrived," he said. "We'll let them speak."

Tina moved forward and said, "Thank you, Nimhi."

Tina motioned for Kim to stand beside her, then said, "I want to introduce you to my sister Kim. As you know, we've been petitioning the leaders in Paradise to open a way for your baptisms and other temple ordinance to be done before the Second Coming. This would allow you to move to Paradise and then come forth on the morning of the First Resurrection. I'm happy to report that the leaders have accepted our proposal to have Kim organize and prepare your names to be completed in the temples of New Jerusalem."

A huge cheer poured down upon them from the group, and Tina smiled at her sister. Kim was overwhelmed by the outpouring of emotion. Many people had tears in their eyes and several others called out, "Thank you, thank you!"

The sisters stayed only a little while longer, before departing to a standing ovation. As they soared away, Tina said to her sister, "No pressure, right?"

Kim smiled. "Oh, I'll be fine, but that's a lot of people! I'm hoping you already have their records somewhere."

"We do," Tina said. "Their records no longer exist on earth, but they've been compiled here. That's our next stop."

They flew to one of the Inca temples on the outskirts of the city, and Tina led Kim to a room that held a desk and a computer. Tina sat down at the keyboard and called up a pedigree chart filled with names. Their mother Miriam was listed on the first line. Tina then stood and motioned for Kim to sit at the computer.

"This is mom's family line," Tina said. "I'm going to set it in motion, and you just need to concentrate. Your spirit will remember this information, and when you return to earth, the Holy Ghost will help you recall what you see."

Tina then hit a button and thousands of names, dates, and places began flashing across the screen. Kim focused on them, and to her amazement, she was able to acknowledge and remember each bit of information. It wasn't long before the images stopped. Kim looked up at her sister and asked, "Is that it?"

"Yep, you're ready to go. When you return, open up your family history program and type in the information as it comes into your mind. Well, I'm afraid it's time to get you back home."

For the first time on her journey, Kim felt sad. "It's so peaceful here, and I love being with you. But I know I've got an important assignment to complete."

Then an idea struck her. "Maybe this is asking too much, but before I go back, can I please see Josh?"

Tina hesitated. "We need to get you back to your body soon, but it wouldn't hurt to ask."

Tina paused as if she is listening to a voice that Kim couldn't hear, and then she nodded and smiled.

"Yes, a brief visit to see Josh has been approved."

They immediately left the Inca temple and within a few moments they burst back through the veil. They zipped across the earth, and as they slowed down above Jerusalem, Kim could see the Dome of the Rock on the Temple Mount.

Just for fun, Tina took Kim zooming through a set of arches in front of the dome. There was some cloud cover, but the golden dome shined brightly in the morning sun. The sisters then glided over the city, and Tina said, "Josh should be somewhere on this street."

They turned a corner and found Josh and Colton walking toward a group of people. Kim rushed to Josh's side, but he didn't seem to notice her as he bent down and talked to a young mother holding a baby girl that was covered with sores. Josh asked if he could bless the child, and then he placed his hands on the baby's head and gave her a blessing. Within seconds the sores seemed to evaporate, replaced with healthy skin. Everyone gasped with happiness, and Josh moved on to another ailing child.

Kim looked at Tina and said, "Thank you for letting me see him. I know he's doing a great work."

Tina motioned above them. "Don't worry. He's in good hands."

Kim looked up and saw several angels following the two apostles, keeping them safe. Tina then took Kim's hand and said, "It's time for you to return to your body. See you soon. I love you!"

In a flurry, they zoomed back across the earth and left the sun behind as they returned to the dark night of New Jerusalem.

Kim awoke on her bed with a jolt. She looked at the clock on the wall. She figured only about three minutes had passed since she'd left her body. She shivered as she rubbed her arms and legs, longing for the warmth she felt in the Spirit World.

"Wow, we sure crammed a lot into those three minutes," she said to herself. "Imagine what could be done in three hours or three days."

It took a little while, but once she felt halfway normal again, she stood up and checked on the twins, who were sleeping soundly. She was now wide awake and felt an urgency to begin working on her new assignment.

She went to her computer, opened up her family history program, and clicked on her personal pedigree chart. She found the end of the line on her mother's side and immediately knew what the next name should be. Her fingers were flying as she began entering names and dates. She knew it would take weeks or even months to get it all done, but she could literally see the pedigree charts and family group sheets in her head.

"Thank thee, Heavenly Father," she said. "I'll do my best."

CHAPTER 15

Mitko Petrov was exhausted both in body and in spirit. He couldn't escape the constant stench of death. It had been nearly three weeks since the horrific horsefly attack, and the number of dead in Moscow alone was in the tens of thousands, with more than four million people dead across Asia and Europe. The bites were terribly lethal, with the majority of those who had been bitten eventually succumbing to the disease.

All healthy men in Moscow were required to help bury the dead in mass graves, and Mitko found himself in the midst of this. He had seen many terrible things in his short life, but this ranked at the top of the list. The condition of the bodies was almost indescribable. Even worse, the bodies essentially fell apart when they were moved. The horseflies that had caused the problem were now gone, but ordinary houseflies were now buzzing everywhere.

Mitko wore overalls, a gas mask and thick rubber gloves to avoid actual contact with the bodies, but it was still almost too much for him to endure. He knew there had been terrible atrocities heaped upon the Russian people in the past, such as Stalin's Great Purge in the late 1930s, and this situation was definitely comparable.

His life had become mind-numbingly repetitive—wake up, eat a meager breakfast, help retrieve and bury dead bodies throughout the day, catch a few hours of sleep, then start the process over again.

The death toll among the Coalition leaders in particular was extremely high. The timing of the outdoor dinner had been an outright catastrophe for them. Both the Russian and the Iranian leaders had died from their infected sores about a week after the attack. If the swarm had come earlier in the day when the leaders had all been indoors, fewer would have died, but Mitko sensed it was the Lord's will to remove so many corrupt men at one time.

Three weeks after the attack, Mitko was summoned to Elias' apartment. Like Mitko, Elias had left the outdoor reception early and had been in a sheltered room when the swarm arrived. He had received just a couple of bites and was now fully recovered.

As Mitko took a seat on a couch, Elias pulled up a chair in front of him. "I'll be convening a meeting of the Coalition leaders tomorrow, and I want you to be there."

Mitko looked closely at Elias. "What are you saying? Have you taken a leadership role with the Coalition?"

Elias nodded. "I've been approached by several of the remaining leaders, and they're offering me a spot at the head of the Coalition. The leaders feel that since I'm not an elected representative, I'll be able to make wise and unbiased decisions. Plus, I do truly desire world peace."

"I agree with their choice," Mitko said. "You're a natural leader, and after the devastation caused by the swarm, it seems everyone just wants to put aside the fighting and get life back to normal."

"That's exactly what I want," Elias said, "but I'll need a trusted assistant who is also wise and unbiased. I know you were close to our Russian friend, and before his death he told me how much he trusted you. If you're willing, I'd like for you to fill that same advisory role for me."

Mitko was surprised and flattered by the invitation. "I'm very honored. Yes, I'd be happy to be your assistant."

Elias smiled. "I know we'll work well together."

At the Coalition meeting, Mitko took his usual seat on the podium, but now he sat next to Elias rather than the departed Russian leader. Once everyone was seated, Elias stood before the group, and his image was shown on large screens on both sides of the room. He looked very impressive in his white robe, clean-shaven face and pony-tailed long hair.

"I come before you as a humbled man, grateful for the privilege to be a part of this remarkable group of leaders, "Elias said solemnly. "I accept your offer to serve as the head of the Coalition. I take this position reluctantly, but I believe we all have the same goal at this time of achieving world peace, and this will be my main objective."

The group applauded loudly, and as they did so, Elias motioned toward Mitko. "I want you to know that Mitko Petrov will serve as my assistant. Before our great Russian leader passed away, he recommended to me that I take advantage of Mitko's wisdom. I look forward to serving with him."

Elias then spoke for several minutes about certain policies the Coalition had been working on before the swarm had arrived, and then he concluded by saying, "World peace is achievable, and I foresee a united global community. This might require us to persuade some non-Coalition nations to our way of thinking. Conflicts may arise, but as future historians look upon our accomplishments they will say those battles were for the greater good as they enjoy a utopian society. Thank you again for this opportunity."

Elias returned to his seat amid thunderous applause, and Mitko applauded as well, but something hadn't felt right to him about Elias' last statements. Under all the sugar-coated words, it sounded like Elias was saying the Coalition would achieve world peace at all costs, even through armed conflict if necessary.

Elias returned to his apartment and wasn't surprised to see an old friend standing in the living room waiting for him. This friend had first visited him a few years ago, soon after he had completed his tour of college campuses in the United States. At the time, this friend had made a promise that seemed impossible. He claimed he could make Elias the most powerful man on earth.

Elias initially resisted his friend's offer, but soon his ego prevailed and he decided to listen to the proposal. As they had talked, the opportunities this friend presented were so enticing that Elias didn't see how he could lose. So the pair had begun meeting occasionally, and Elias would follow his friend's instructions. Now only a few years later, Elias was truly on the verge of becoming the world's most powerful man.

"Well done today," the friend said. "Sometimes you really remind me of myself."

"Thank you," Elias said. "I'll take that as a compliment."

His friend laughed. "I would hope so."

Elias fully understood who he was dealing with. At first he was troubled with the fact he had "made a deal with the devil" but in a twisted way, he truly felt Satan was looking out for his best interests. Together, they would produce global peace and make the world a better place for all humanity.

"My only concern was you didn't mention a timetable in your speech," Satan said. "We had discussed that the time has come to eliminate Israel, but you didn't mention it to the other leaders."

"I have thought a lot about that," Elias responded. "Wouldn't it be better to let Israel dig its own grave by continuing to resist our invitations to join the Coalition? If we strengthen all of the surrounding countries first, then they won't have a chance. Eventually Israel will do something foolish and then we can crush them without it looking like we wanted to do so all along."

Satan frowned. "You really don't understand, do you? We're running out of time. Don't worry about strengthening those other nations. We really only have one enemy—the Latter-day Saints."

"The Mormons?" Elias asked. "They're not a threat."

Satan moved closer to Elias, glaring at him. "You've met those two apostles in Jerusalem. You sensed the power they hold. That power is real, and they could overthrow everything the Coalition has accomplished. They are growing stronger and more confident. Your first goal should be to kill them, and then occupy Israel. After that, you can worry about the rest of the world."

"Actually, I was hoping to persuade those apostles to our way of thinking," Elias said. "I've never met a man who can't be tempted somehow. Wouldn't it be marvelous to have them working on our side?"

"Yes, it would, but there's no chance they would join us."

"Are you sure?" Elias asked. "If we invited them here to the Kremlin and offered them anything in the world, you don't think they'd be interested?"

Satan shook his head. "No. I agree that nearly every man can eventually be worn down by temptation, but not these two. I've thrown everything at them since they were young men, and they've hardly flinched. They'd laugh in your face if you offered them a position in the Coalition. Eliminating them really is our best option."

"Okay, but I don't think the other Coalition leaders are in the mood to make an unprovoked attack on Jerusalem," Elias said. "The Israelis would have to do something horrific to stir up enough support."

"That shouldn't be difficult," Satan said. "We both know there's one target that would cause enough worldwide outrage. Simply destroy the Dome of the Rock, but make it appear as if the Jews did it."

Elias began to smile as he pondered that suggestion. He had extensive contacts throughout the Middle East, and several groups came to mind who would be thrilled to perform the attack.

"There's a group of extremists in Libya who might be best suited for such a task," Elias said. "They could easily slip inside Israel's borders and fire missiles from within a few miles of Jerusalem. I'll contact them right away. It could happen within a day."

"Excellent," Satan said. "That brings me to another matter. I know you see yourself as a great deceiver, but you've been deceived yourself. Your new assistant isn't who he pretends to be."

"You mean Mitko? I haven't detected anything out of order with him. He has always been straightforward with me."

Satan frowned. "Oh, he hasn't really lied to you, but there's a chance he could alert the outside world about your plans. He's a

Latter-day Saint, just like those two apostles, and he has connections to them."

Elias was astonished. "I can hardly believe it."

He felt betrayed and was ready to rush to Mitko's room and confront him, but Satan held up his hands and told him to calm down.

"Let's not ruin this opportunity," Satan said. "There's a way we can frame Mitko concerning the attack on Israel and solidify the evidence against the Jews at the same time. Grab a pen and paper, and I'll tell you what to write."

Elias was soon jotting down the words that were coming from his master's mouth. As he wrote the final words, they both couldn't resist laughing with pleasure. Elias paused to read through it, and he laughed again.

"This will be the final piece of the puzzle," Elias said to the dark spirit hovering next to him. "You know, sometimes you really do amaze me."

"Just chalk it up to many years of experience—and a brilliant mind," Satan said. "Now hide that note somewhere safe until the right time, and contact your friends in Libya today."

CHAPTER 16

Two days later, Josh and Colton were walking through the Old City of Jerusalem. The healings they had performed had softened the hearts of many people, and the apostles were now teaching the basic principles of the gospel to several groups throughout the day with the approval of Benjamin Cohen.

Out of the corner of his eye, Colton saw a flash of light. He turned to see a missile racing across the sky.

"Josh, look at that!"

The apostles watched in astonishment as the missile plunged down and burst through the roof of the Dome of the Rock. An enormous explosion followed, ripping the golden dome apart. Two more missiles followed the same flight path, each one inflicting greater damage. By the time the dust settled a few minutes later, a pile of smoking rubble stood where the magnificent dome had once stood. Fragments of the dome were now scattered all over the surrounding neighborhood.

People came out of their homes at the sound of the explosions, and as they caught sight of the rubble, they shrieked in terror and hurried back inside. They all knew that dark times were coming.

The apostles ran toward the Temple Mount, passing people who were running away from the scene. As they got closer, it was clear there had been many casualties accompanying the destruction of the building.

A woman they had met a few days earlier came up to them. "My children are buried under a pile of stones," she cried. "I can hear their screams, but I can't reach them."

"Take us to them," Josh said. "We'll do what we can."

The woman led them to the base of the temple mount. "My children had gone to climb the steps to the Dome of the Rock while I sat on a bench here below. Then I heard the first explosion, and the steps were buried!"

Josh reached the stones, and it looked eerily similar to the pile of rocks he had moved with Mathoni to uncover the bus in the Arizona desert.

He prayed in his mind, "Heavenly Father, am I allowed to use my priesthood at this time to save these children?"

Josh immediately felt a warm confirmation from the Holy Ghost that it would be acceptable, so he motioned for Colton to join him at the pile.

"I'm going to use the priesthood to move these stones one at a time," Josh told him. "I need you to stay close to the pile and point to the stones that I should move to reach the children."

Colton nodded. He was fully aware of Josh's previous uses of the priesthood, both in Arizona and then to raise the land bridge that had allowed the Lost Ten Tribes to cross the Bering Strait.

"Sounds good," Colton said. "Let me see what we're facing."

He climbed onto the pile and listened for the cries of the trapped children. He disappeared down into the pile, then emerged and said, "I can see them, but you'll need to move all these stones in front to get them out."

Josh prayed once again for help, then as he pointed at a stone, it began to move out of the way. There were nearly a hundred people watching, and they gasped in surprise as Josh guided four stones away from the pile. As he lowered the last one to the ground, Colton scrambled into the opening that had been created.

He quickly emerged again. "Josh, come see what we're facing. The kids are still behind a giant rock, but I don't see how you can safely move it."

Josh studied how the rocks were wedged against each other. It was like playing a giant game of Jenga, and removing that one stone could cause the entire pile to tumble down on the children.

"Let me try something," Josh said. "It scares me to even think about, but if I can lift that rock off the ground a couple of feet, the kids could crawl underneath it to safety."

Josh prayed fervently for assistance from heaven, then he used the priesthood to slowly inch that stone upward. He soon had it about 18 inches off the ground, but the rocks stacked on top of it began to shift.

"That's as high as I dare to go," Josh told Colton. "See if they can climb through."

Josh's forehead was covered in sweat, and in some ways it felt more difficult to hold that stone in place with his mind than if he was doing it with his bare hands. He could hear Colton encouraging the children to slide through the opening, and within a few moments Colton stood up holding a small girl. Following behind him were two young boys. Their mother rushed forward in tears, and Colton handed the girl to her.

"Thank you so much," she told Colton as she hugged all of the children.

Josh slowly lowered the stone back to the ground and then joined them. The woman gave him a hug and said, "I wouldn't have believed it if I hadn't seen it myself, but thank you, thank you, thank you!"

The news of the miraculous rescue spread like wildfire, and soon other people crowded around the apostles to ask for their help rescuing others who were trapped on the Temple Mount. The apostles stayed busy throughout the day, working together to lift stones and rescue several other people. Some of the people were injured, and at times the apostles would pause and lay their hands on the heads of the afflicted people and heal them. They healed many men, women and children of all faiths and nationalities, which helped them gain favor in the eyes of everyone who witnessed their miracles.

As the people would thank them, the apostles always made it clear that the miracles came from God, and that they were merely instruments in his hands. So while the destruction of the dome was a horrible event, the apostles were grateful for the opportunity to bless the lives of the some of Heavenly Father's children.

After an hour of helping rescue people through the power of the priesthood, the apostles were summoned to Benjamin Cohen's house to discuss the situation. They found Benjamin sitting at a table with several other Jewish leaders.

"Welcome, my friends," Benjamin said wearily. "We've heard of the miracles you have performed, and we're very grateful for your service in our behalf. We know God is with you."

"Thank you," Colton said. "You know we're here to help you however we can."

"We appreciate that, and we'll certainly need your help in the days ahead. That's why I invited you here."

"What information do you have about the attack?" Josh asked. "Who fired the missiles?"

Benjamin shook his head. "We don't know, other than we're certain it wasn't us. But the problem is those missiles were launched from within our borders."

"That's not good," Colton said. "It won't take long for the rest of the world to start blaming Israel for the attack, whether it's justified or not."

"Exactly," Benjamin said. "We're surprised there hasn't already been some sort of retaliatory strike from one of the Muslim nations, but we've received reports that nearly all of our remaining Muslim residents have actually fled the country in fear that they'll be blown to pieces. They're crossing over into Lebanon and Syria, and I'm guessing those countries have asked the Coalition to allow these people to escape before launching an attack."

"So is anybody staying?" Colton asked.

"Well, as far as we can tell, only the Jews, because we don't have anywhere else to go."

Josh looked Benjamin straight in the eyes. "I promise you we won't abandon you. In fact, I would like to request that Elder Negus and I be allowed to live on the Temple Mount."

The other leaders in the room expressed surprise at his request, but Josh added, "It will mainly serve the purpose of being able to have a good view of the city as we seek to protect it. God will keep us safe."

Benjamin nodded. "That will work. We'll be organizing the residents at our synagogues and preparing them for what's coming. At the very least, I expect the Coalition to put a total siege on our borders, so we need to gather all of our food into central locations, and also move the people into underground shelters in case of a broader attack."

"That's very wise," Josh said. "Be sure to ask the people to pray to God that the country can be preserved. At this point, it might be our only hope."

CHAPTER 17

Back in the Kremlin, as soon as Elias had received confirmation from his secret sources in Libya that the Dome of the Rock had been destroyed, he announced an emergency meeting to be held that afternoon for all of the Coalition leaders. He purposely didn't tell them what had occurred, hoping to create a major emotional impact when he shared the news.

As the leaders filed into the meeting room, Elias stood quietly at the podium. As the final person took his seat, Elias began, "I've received information that will likely change each of our lives. My sources are reporting that three missiles were fired from southern Israel toward Jerusalem. These missiles have completely demolished the Dome of the Rock."

His words first brought stunned silence, then a unified cry of outrage. Several leaders accused the Jews of being behind the attack, and they called for immediate retaliatory strikes on all known Jewish outposts.

Other leaders were opposed to retaliation bombings for the sake of preserving Jerusalem. Representatives from Muslim countries didn't want additional historic buildings and sites to be needlessly destroyed.

One official said, "We don't want to turn Jerusalem into piles of rubble, we just want to eliminate the Jews. So let's send in ground troops to take care of the problem."

Several other leaders voiced their agreement, while others still wanted an immediate strike on Jewish sites. Elias let them argue back and forth for another few minutes, but then he got them to settle down a little by saying, "I'm as angry as you are, but we can't act hastily. We don't have definite proof that the Jews are involved. We're doing everything we can to determine who is behind the attack. As I said, our preliminary reports indicate the missiles were fired from within Israel's borders, but we don't want to make any accusations until there's more information."

Some leaders continued to argue, but Elias held up his hands and said, "I've also received reports that tens of thousands of Muslims are now leaving Israel, and at the very least we should give them time to escape, rather than needlessly kill them. Although it looks like the Jews are involved, we should at least speak with their leaders and hear their side of the story."

Elias' comments made sense to most of the leaders, and a vote was taken to hold off on any drastic action until more information was available.

Mitko had silently listened to Elias speak to the group. He was completely shocked by the news of the attack, partly because he knew this event would likely put the two apostles in Jerusalem in great danger. Once the meeting concluded, he walked back to his apartment in a daze. He knew if the Jews truly were somehow involved, the Coalition wouldn't hesitate to destroy Israel, and he wouldn't be able to stop it.

About an hour after the meeting, Elias went alone to Mitko's apartment and gently knocked on the door. Mitko opened it and was surprised to see his visitor, who rarely went anywhere without at least one guard at his side.

"Come in," Mitko said, motioning to two stools at a table in the kitchen. "I'm sorry I don't have much in terms of furniture."

"That's all right. I just wanted to see how you were doing," Elias said. "During our meeting you seemed quite disturbed by the news about the Dome of the Rock."

Mitko shrugged. "I'm just really surprised, because it really appears the Israelis were behind it. I just can't believe they would be so foolish. They had to know it would anger every Arab nation and probably lead to a Coalition attack."

"I agree with you," Elias said. "But let me switch gears for a moment. May I ask you a personal question?"

Mitko glanced quickly into Elias' eyes. "I suppose."

"Someone told me you believe in Jesus Christ. Is that true?"

Mitko felt a chill rush through his body. "That's a strange question."

Elias got right in his face. "Answer me! Yes or no?"

There was silence for nearly ten seconds as the men stared at each other. Finally Mitko said, "Yes."

"Wrong answer."

Elias grabbed Mitko roughly by the hair and slammed him to the floor. He put his knee in Mitko's chest and slapped him hard across the face.

"Either deny Jesus Christ or die!" Elias hissed as he pulled a small knife from his robe.

"Jesus lives. I'll never deny it," Mitko said, his eyes bulging at the sight of the weapon.

"Then I have no use for you."

Elias quickly plunged the blade into Mitko's chest and twisted it through his heart. Mitko cried out in agony and tried to sit up, but then his head slumped to the floor.

Elias stood motionless for more than a minute, watching the blood seep out of Mitko's chest. He finally checked Mitko's vital signs. There was no sign of breathing or a pulse, so he pulled the blade from Mitko's body and went to the kitchen sink, where he rinsed off the knife and dried his hands. Then he took an envelope from inside his robe and removed a handwritten note from it. He unfolded the note and placed it on the kitchen table near Mitko's body.

For a slight moment Elias panicked as he realized the note was in his own handwriting, but he knew it really wouldn't matter once everything was set in motion. He returned to the kitchen and retrieved the knife.

He grimaced slightly before using the knife to slice open the palm of his own left hand, drawing blood. He quickly put the knife back inside the wound in Mitko's chest before exiting the apartment, leaving the door partially open as he departed.

Mitko's spirit had left his body almost immediately after the knife penetrated his heart, sparing him prolonged pain. He hovered in the corner of the room, watching Elias methodically move around the apartment. It was clear that the attack had been planned. Once Elias left the apartment, Mitko moved toward the table to look at the note. It read:

To Benjamin Cohen,
Congratulations on destroying the Dome of the Rock. That is a major step forward in our efforts to rebuild the Jewish temple on the Temple Mount. I know you were worried about retaliation from the Coalition, but I assure you that Elias is pushing toward achieving global peace. I don't feel the Coalition will do anything besides give Israel a strong reprimand. I recommend that you take the reprimand graciously, but then continue your efforts with the two apostles to strengthen the army. As I mentioned, the Coalition is not being aggressive at this time, so let's make the most of it. I'll continue to monitor the Coalition's intentions and let you know if there are any changes.
I'm confident the Latter-day Saints and the Jews will triumph!
Your brother,
Mitko Petrov

"What a horrible lie," Mitko shouted. He didn't even know anyone named Benjamin Cohen. He tried to grab the note so he could rip it up, but his spirit hand simply kept passing through the paper. Within a few moments there was a commotion in the hall, and Mitko went to see what was happening. Elias' personal bodyguard was hurrying toward the apartment with Elias right behind him, holding his bleeding hand.

"This is the room?" the guard asked.

"Yes," Elias said. "I came to talk to Mitko about the bombing of the Dome of the Rock, and I found him folding up a note. I asked to see it, but he got really defensive about it. When I tried to take the note from him, he lunged at me with a knife. I blocked it with my hand, but he still got me pretty good."

Elias held his bleeding hand toward the guard, who said, "Yeah, that looks like it hurts."

"I'll probably need stitches. Anyway, after we struggled for a few seconds, I wrestled the knife away from him. At that point I felt I had no choice but to defend myself."

"That's understandable," the guard said. "I wish we had been here with you."

"That's fine," Elias said. "I've always felt perfectly safe with Mitko, so I'm as surprised as anyone that he attacked me."

The guard looked at the paper on the table. "Is that the note you're talking about?"

"Yes. Go ahead and read it."

The guard took a few moments to read it, then said, "That's terrible. What a traitor!"

Elias nodded. "I'm completely stunned. I need to let the other leaders know we've been infiltrated by the Jews."

Mitko stayed near his body following his death, and he watched as Elias' bodyguard and another man took the body on a stretcher to a vacant field outside the Kremlin walls. They stopped near a mound of dirt that looked quite fresh, then set the body down and quickly dug a shallow grave. Mitko continued to feel a mixture of anger and betrayal, and he noticed other spirits hovering nearby who shared the same feelings. He realized this vacant field was actually a burial ground for people who had been "eliminated" for the sake of the Coalition.

However, once his body had been put to rest, Mitko suddenly felt a strange sense of contentment. He sensed he had accomplished his mission among the Coalition leaders, and he realized he was still on an assignment from the Lord, whether he was in his mortal body or not.

He quickly traveled back to the Coalition's main meeting room, where Elias stood before the other leaders and repeated the story he had told the guard about how Mitko had attacked him. Elias held up his newly stitched and bandaged hand, then in the other hand he held up the letter for them to see. He read it to them, and their furious reactions were exactly what Elias had hoped for. He slammed his hand down on the podium in disgust and then theatrically crumpled up the letter.

"I'm all for peace and harmony, but it's clear the Jews are plotting against us," Elias said. "I know this man Benjamin Cohen, and he's a real threat to us. I met with him when I visited Jerusalem, and he assured me that the Jews only sought peace, but from this note it's clear he lied to me. This kind of outrage can't be tolerated. For all we know, Mitko Petrov already shared most of our plans with his Jewish friends. We have tolerated the Jews and their misguided leaders for long enough. Just as the Dome of the Rock has fallen, so must Israel!"

Elias ordered an army of 100,000 men to be transported into Syria within two days in preparation for an all-out ground assault against Jerusalem that he would personally supervise. He concluded by saying, "Within a week, I'll be standing triumphantly on the Temple Mount, adding one more jewel to our global crown."

The Coalition leaders shouted their approval, and then they began to make more detailed plans.

Mitko knew Israel was on the verge of disaster, and Josh Brown needed to be made aware of what was being planned by the Coalition. Like a flash of light, Mitko bolted out of the room on his way to the BYU Jerusalem Center.

In another corner of the room, Satan noticed Mitko's sudden departure, but he wasn't overly concerned about it. He was still gloating over his latest victory. He had tutored thousands of men over the centuries and turned them into his servants, but this latest conquest ranked among his most cherished ones of the past century, right up there with Lenin, Stalin, Hitler, and Mao.

Gaining Elias' soul was even more meaningful to Satan because while those other men were already somewhat evil in their own right, Elias had started out with that annoying Light of Christ in his eyes. Satan admitted to himself there were times when he wasn't sure Elias would fully commit to his cause. It had taken years of patient guidance to reach this point, but when Elias sunk that knife into Mitko's chest, the battle was won. The stabbing had sent the same thrill through Satan as when Cain had slain his brother Abel.

"I finally have my Antichrist," Satan said with a twisted grin. "Those apostles don't have a chance against him."

CHAPTER 18

Moments later, Mitko was standing next to Josh Brown in the BYU Jerusalem Center as the two apostles packed up a few final items to take to their new home on the Temple Mount.

"Josh, I need to talk to you," Mitko shouted, tapping Josh hard on the shoulder.

Josh suddenly stood up straight and looked around. It almost felt like he had a mosquito buzzing in his ear, but then the buzzing formed into words. "Josh, this is Mitko Petrov," the voice said. "I've been killed, and I have a message for you."

Josh turned to Colton and said, "We have a visitor. Let's sit quietly on the couch."

Colton raised his eyebrows, but he sat down next to Josh. Once they were settled and silent, Mitko's spirit materialized before them.

"Hello, my dear friend," Josh said quietly. "Colton, this is Mitko Petrov, who has been serving among the Coalition leaders. Since you are here, I guess it didn't end well."

"I've been killed, but it was meant to be," Mitko said before explaining to them how Elias had risen to power. Then he asked, "Do you know Benjamin Cohen? He is mentioned in a note Elias is using to justify an attack on Israel."

"We do," Josh said. "He's one of the top Jewish leaders here in Jerusalem."

"That explains a lot," Mitko said. He then told them what Elias' note had said, and the apostles exchanged worried looks.

"This could be disastrous for us," Josh said. "If Elias has

convinced the Coalition leaders that the Jews are responsible for the dome's destruction, they'll have plenty of motivation to destroy Israel."

"Exactly," Mitko said. "Elias plans to lead an army into Israel from Syria within two days, and then they'll just methodically crush any Israeli opposition."

Josh got a determined look on his face. "We can't let it happen. We need to get to the Temple Mount as soon as possible."

Colton nodded grimly. "I'm ready when you are."

"Thank you," Mitko said. "I knew I could count on both of you to stop them."

With his message delivered, Mitko began to fade away. Then with a brief wave, he vanished.

✢ ✢ ✢

The apostles soon journeyed to the Temple Mount, arriving just before sunset. During their earlier visit to the Temple Mount, Colton had noticed a small building covered with debris that was still usable. The building would work well for the apostles as a place to sleep and store their supplies. They didn't need much else, since they intended to be out among the people most of the time.

The building had two small beds inside it, and the men endured a restless night's sleep. They knew the Lord wanted them on the Temple Mount, but in the back of their minds they knew the site had been bombed less than 24 hours earlier.

The next morning they knelt together to plead with the Lord for protection and guidance in the tasks that lay before them. As they prayed, a discernible glow began to descend through the ceiling above them. Within seconds, the Lord Jesus Christ stood in the room, hovering just off the ground. His glory was almost overwhelming, and both apostles instinctively bowed down before the Savior.

"Blessed art thou, my beloved apostles," the Savior said. "I am pleased with your efforts yesterday in saving the lives of many people. You are fulfilling your assignments well."

Josh looked up. "Thank thee, dear Savior, but I still feel so inadequate. Please bless us with the power to do thy will."

"I know the feelings of thy hearts, and that is why I am here," the Savior said. "Thou hast sought to always keep my commandments, and I shall make thee mighty in word and in deed. All things shall be done unto thee according to thy word, for I know thou shalt not ask that which is contrary to my will."

The Savior smiled and added, "I declare it unto thee, in the presence of mine angels, that I give unto you both the power that whatsoever ye shall seal on earth shall be sealed in heaven; and whatsoever ye shall loose on earth shall be loosed in heaven; and thus shall ye have power among this people."

"Thank thee, dear Lord," Colton said softly. "We are thy servants and only seek to build up thy kingdom."

"I know. There are more plagues coming, but I shall lighten their effect here in Jerusalem, while increasing the effect on your enemies. Devote your time to helping Benjamin Cohen build the temple. They have the materials ready, but they'll need your assistance."

Josh needed a little clarification. "Just to be sure, we can use this sealing power however we see fit, as long as it accomplishes a righteous purpose?"

"That is right," the Savior said. "But your two main objectives are to help build the temple and to defend Jerusalem against any attacks."

The Savior then beckoned for them to stand. He embraced each one of them and thanked them again for their service.

"Your wives and children are being watched over, and everything is well in Zion," the Savior said. "The end is growing close, and then you'll be reunited with them again."

"This temple will resemble the previous Jewish temples, right?" Josh asked.

"Yes, make sure the Jewish leaders build it after the manner described in the Book of Ezekiel. There will come a day when another temple will be built in Jerusalem that is similar to the modern temples, but that one will not be built until it is needed."

"Once the Millennium begins?" Colton asked.

"That is correct," the Savior said. "The time is fast approaching when the Jews will finally accept their Messiah and Friend, and the construction of this first temple will help prepare them for that day."

The Savior gave them a final smile, then he departed as quickly as he had come, but the Lord's embrace had given the apostles the confidence to face any challenge that lay ahead. They looked at each other, still filled with wonderment at what had transpired.

After the Savior departed, the apostles felt physically and spiritually drained, and they rested on their beds for several minutes discussing the experience.

"His words sounded similar to something I recently read in the Book of Mormon," Colton said as he grabbed his scriptures from one of his bags and started flipping the pages. "Ah, here it is in Helaman chapter 10, where the Savior gave the sealing power to the prophet Nephi."

Colton read aloud the first 11 verses of the chapter, and then the apostles were silent, hardly able to comprehend the blessings they had received. Finally Josh said, "Let's always strengthen each other and never falter. Together we can accomplish the Lord's will."

Later that morning Benjamin Cohen sent a group of Israeli soldiers to meet with the apostles and organize a communications system that could be used throughout the region. The soldiers proposed using a code that relayed information via mirrors. They didn't want to risk the chance of their messages being intercepted on the radio, and they fully expected the Coalition to cut off their electrical supply anyway.

The apostles liked the idea, and the soldiers agreed to divide into groups that would be stationed atop several major hills all the way to the Syrian border. Any advancement of the Coalition army into Israel could immediately be reported through this system.

By noon the soldiers began traveling to the various locations, hoping to be in place before the Coalition forces crossed the border. The apostles had three Israeli soldiers stationed with them who were experts in both sending and deciphering the code.

The next morning, the first points of light came from a nearby mountain top. One of the soldiers spoke as the flashes were received.

"The Coalition army crossed the Syrian border this morning," the soldier said. "They're making good speed on the highway, and they're already near the city of Nazareth."

"Whoa, they're coming fast," Josh said. He knew Nazareth was about 65 miles north of Jerusalem, which was way too close for comfort. "I better put up a roadblock."

The sky was mostly clear, but Josh looked at the sky and commanded a tornado to form just south of Nazareth. A menacing dark cloud quickly thickened out of nowhere, and a thin funnel soon descended to the ground.

"No," Josh said. "I need an F5 tornado." He then commanded the storm to increase to maximum intensity, and the funnel quickly expanded into a swirling giant a mile across and thousands of feet high. The apostles were too far away to see any actual destruction, but a message was soon relayed by the mirror operators.

"The soldiers near Nazareth report that the tornado touched down right in front of the army," the soldier said as he watched a mirror on a nearby hill flash a series of messages. "They have stopped their vehicles and are scattering."

"Very good," Josh said. "But that's not enough to stop them."

Josh then commanded the tornado to move steadily north, and the reports started coming in rapidly from two different peaks.

"Massive destruction among the Coalition troops . . . tanks and jeeps are overturned . . . the tornado is actually chasing the soldiers back up the highway and some of them are being sucked into it."

Josh simply nodded and allowed the tornado to stay on the ground for a few more minutes to really put a damper on the army's plans, then he finally commanded the storm to go away. The soldiers watched in awe as the funnel retreated into the sky, and the clouds dissipated.

Elias rolled over and spat grains of sand out of his mouth as he watched the tornado vanish. He had been slammed hard in the left shoulder by flying debris soon after the tornado touched down, knocking him completely out of the jeep. He had landed hard on his right shoulder, leaving him partly buried in the sand along the road. He tried to sit up, but a searing pain shot through the palm of his left hand.

"Oww," he cried, looking down to see that the stitches had ripped out in the cut he'd inflicted on himself after he killed Mitko. The wound was now bleeding heavily, and he finally tore off part of his robe to wrap it tightly.

Elias slowly stood and surveyed the chaotic scene surrounding him. The jeep he had been riding in was overturned thirty yards down the road, and Elias could see the body of his driver pinned beneath it. He approached the jeep and it was obvious the driver was dead.

The Coalition's vehicles were scattered everywhere except on the road where they belonged, and he knew their casualties were going to be high. He had actually seen several soldiers being sucked out of the transport trucks into the tornado, and he had no hope they had survived.

Elias groaned audibly, feeling frustrated by the unavoidable delay the tornado had caused. He had hoped to catch the Jews by surprise and actually conquer Jerusalem that very day, but now those hopes were ruined.

As he joined a few other soldiers and listened to their reports, it was clear the army wouldn't be going anywhere until all of the damage had been assessed. It would take several hours to even determine which soldiers had survived.

"There was nothing normal about that tornado," Elias said

angrily to himself as he looked at the blue sky. "The apostles are behind this, and they need to be stopped."

Elias began marching back up the road toward Nazareth, shouting for his soldiers to gather together, check the vehicles, and begin repairing the damage.

CHAPTER 19

Elias had started the day with 100,000 men under his command, but after making a head count throughout the army's divisions, it was estimated that nearly 15,000 of his soldiers had been killed by the tornado, and another 5,000 were simply missing—most likely swept up and carried so far away that their bodies hadn't been found.

The storm had been particularly brutal on the army's transport trucks that had been carrying the soldiers. There were axles strewn along the road, and even the trucks that were in pretty good shape had their windshields smashed in. So in order to continue the attack on Jerusalem, the majority of the soldiers would have to walk the rest of the way. Despite all of these obstacles, Elias gathered together the army's leaders and urged them to move forward.

"Yes, we've suffered casualties, and we're now less equipped than we were, but we still have the element of surprise," Elias told them. "Even as depleted as we are, we could easily conquer the Jews."

The other leaders listened quietly, then a top general said, "I understand the element of surprise, but what's the hurry? We can go back to Syria, get reorganized and patch up our wounds, then be back on the attack within a few days. The Jews aren't going anywhere."

The other leaders shared their opinions, and Elias realized that while they were trying to be diplomatic and not offend him, everyone agreed with the general. For the sake of keeping harmony, Elias finally said the army should return to Syria, but deep down he knew they were missing a huge opportunity. He still sensed those two apostles were somehow behind the tornado, as illogical as it seemed. They would feel they'd gained a major victory and would grow more confident in their abilities to withstand the Coalition forces.

The other reason Elias wanted the army to continue on to Jerusalem was because he knew Satan wasn't going to be happy with him. He had never seen Satan really throw a tantrum yet, but he felt he was going to witness one after this failed effort.

Elias' own anger was mounting, because all of this nonsense about Israel could all be over so quickly. He had the capability to unleash a nuclear weapon on Jerusalem and just be done with it, but there were too many variables involved. A nuclear attack on the area—or a major bombing attack of any type—would destroy numerous historical sites that were sacred to many different religions and ethnic groups throughout the Coalition nations. If Elias authorized such an attack, he would likely lose all of their support, so a traditional battle using soldiers was the only real option at the moment.

Elias finally took a deep breath and told himself, "You're still in good shape. Everyone still thinks the Jews destroyed the Dome of the Rock. Just be patient."

Jerusalem's residents spent a sleepless night waiting for an attack from the Coalition army. The word had spread throughout the city that the army was near Nazareth, and although the apostles had slowed them down with the tornado, it wasn't clear until sunrise that the army was retreating northward.

Benjamin Cohen came to the Temple Mount to congratulate the apostles on stopping the army. "Even though our armed forces are strong, we wouldn't have been able to halt an army of that size," he told them. "You saved us."

"All the credit goes to our Heavenly Father," Josh said. "I'm sure they'll be back, but we'll be ready for them."

Josh then explained to Benjamin that God had told them the

time had come to build the Jerusalem Temple on the former site of the Dome of the Rock. Benjamin's face showed a mixture of delight and fear.

"Do we dare begin?" he asked. "All it would take is another missile strike to destroy all of our efforts."

Josh put his hand on his friend's shoulder. "Don't worry. We'll assist you and protect you. God wants the temple built, and I know it can be done."

"I appreciate your confidence," Benjamin said. "As we discussed during our first meeting together, we already have stones hidden away that are cut to the precise measurements given in the ancient writings of Ezekiel. Now we just need to transport them to the Temple Mount and assemble them."

Josh smiled. "Elder Negus and I are as excited as you to see the temple rise on this spot once again. With your permission, I would like to offer a prayer and consecrate this site to God, and to ask for a blessing that our efforts will prosper."

"Absolutely," Benjamin replied.

Josh then knelt down and encouraged the others to do so as well. Then he poured out his heart to Heavenly Father, dedicating the site of the temple. Afterward, they arose to their feet and basked in the warm spirit had surrounded them.

"God is with us," Benjamin said. "I can feel it."

Three days later the apostles were assisting with the transportation of the foundation stones on large flatbed trailers when Benjamin hurried up to Josh.

"Something really strange is happening," he said with a worried look. "We've been monitoring the radio transmissions from several Coalition countries, and they're all reporting a strange event. They claim that the oceans have turned to blood! I've checked with our leaders in Tel Aviv along the shore of the Mediterranean Sea, and they confirm the same thing."

Josh wasn't completely surprised at the news, but he had

hoped it wouldn't come so soon. After the attack by the swarm of horseflies, the apostles had carefully read the plagues listed in the Book of Revelation, and they knew this event was next on the list of disasters.

Benjamin watched Josh's face, wondering why he didn't seem overly upset by the news. "Aren't you worried?" he asked. "Do you know what it might be?"

"It's the second plague listed by John the Beloved in the New Testament," Josh said. "Do the reports say what's actually happening to the water?"

Benjamin shrugged. "We don't know much yet, but the reports mention it's more drastic than just the ocean water changing color. An actual chemical reaction seems to be taking place. They say it is depositing a rust-like residue along the shore."

That can't be good for the fish," Colton said. "Are there any reports about that?"

"Yes, there are already all kinds of dead fish floating up on the shores, even sharks and whales."

"This is terrible," Josh said. "Please keep us posted on anything else you hear about it."

After an exhausting three-day walk, Elias had just crossed back into Syria with the army when he first received reports from the Kremlin about the latest plague. He had fully intended to quickly reorganize the Coalition army, obtain new vehicles, and launch another attack on Jerusalem within a week, but it was clear the Coalition needed his leadership. He fielded calls from the presidents of several countries, each asking him how they should respond.

Elias was secretly surprised and flattered that they were seeking his opinion, proving his new title actually carried some weight. By the next morning he was in a jet headed to Moscow to handle the situation. The conquest of Jerusalem would have to wait.

When Elias walked into the main Coalition meeting room later that same day, all of the other leaders were already in their seats.

Several scientists had been working around the clock to figure out what was going on in the oceans, and they were now ready to present their preliminary findings.

A Chinese scientist stood before the group and said, "We've pinpointed the location of numerous underwater earthquakes that have occurred during the past week across the globe. These quakes took place at extreme depths, and our initial feeling is that massive amounts of iron and other minerals were released from giant fissures in the ocean floor."

Elias spoke up. "Has this ever happened before?"

The scientist shook his head. "Never on this scale. It's unprecedented for such an occurrence to happen all over the globe at the same time, but from our readings it appears the quakes fed off each other, like a domino effect that traveled throughout the earth. This chain reaction unleashed huge amounts of toxic gases and other minerals. These substances are interfering with the ecosystem and killing the sea life."

A representative from Japan raised his hand. "This event is already destroying my country's economy. All of the fishing villages are affected. At first my people thought they could at least gather up the fish and eat them, but we've heard reports that anyone who eats the fish gets violently ill, and some have died. We're going to have millions of starving citizens to deal with if this continues for very long."

The scientist nodded. "I understand, but we don't know how long it will take for the minerals to settle out. It could take weeks or even months."

His response caused a lot of grumbles from the leaders, and Elias sensed it was time to take charge. He stood up and thanked the scientist, then confidently assured the leaders that all would be well. He asked for each country to first take care of their own people while the Coalition organized a broader effort that would reach out to everyone and help where it was needed most.

"We're exactly what we say we are," Elias declared. "We're a united coalition, and we'll overcome this problem."

After the meeting ended, many delegates came forward to shake Elias' hand and thank him for taking control of the situation. He calmly comforted each of them, but deep down he felt a growing sense of panic. Millions of people were going to die in the next few weeks, and there wasn't anything he could do to prevent it.

Then a strange sense of confidence settled over him as he realized these global catastrophes were stepping stones for him to reach his ultimate goal. With each major problem, his stature among the other leaders was elevated. Even now, he was being recognized as the key person to consult in times of emergency, and if other problems arose, he'd be right there to lead the way.

He knew that leading a conquest of Israel would have brought him fame and respect, but it wouldn't have brought him the long-term recognition and global attention he was gaining now. Defeating Israel was still on his agenda, but it could sit on the backburner for awhile.

Elias suppressed a smile as he shook hands with the remaining leaders. All of the things Satan had promised him seemed to be falling into place.

CHAPTER 20

The prophet frowned as the news reports came in concerning the conditions of the oceans. The First Presidency and most of the Twelve Apostles had gathered in the New Jerusalem Temple to listen to a broadcast originating in England. The Saints had been greatly blessed earlier in the year when one of the technicians in Zion had been able to establish contact with a satellite transmitting radio broadcasts from Europe. It had been a great tool in monitoring what was happening in the rest of the world.

The Church leaders listened intently as the broadcaster gave vivid details of how the Atlantic Ocean had turned bright red and that vast amounts of sea life were washing up on the seashores.

"I don't think there's any doubt now that the seven plagues are underway," the prophet said to the other men. "First came the flies, and now this. I need to inform the Saints of what is happening. Let's announce that I will be addressing the Saints tomorrow morning. We need to broadcast it to every stake center, and then we'll send the transcript of the message to the outlying Cities of Light as well."

The next morning the prophet stood at the podium under the center dome of the New Jerusalem Temple. Every seat was filled, and he knew millions of Saints were gathered in stake centers throughout Zion.

"My dear brothers and sisters, I first want to thank you for your continual service to each other," the prophet began. "I know the

Lord is pleased with each of you, and we have truly developed into a Zion society. Continue on this course and you'll inherit eternal life in the Celestial Kingdom. Besides, I think we've all heard that the Second Coming will happen tomorrow, haven't we?"

The congregation chuckled. Lately there had been rumors spreading through the LDS community that the Savior would return any day.

The prophet then grew serious. "Unfortunately, that isn't the case. We still live in perilous times. There are many prophecies that must be fulfilled before the Savior returns in glory, including what are known as the 'seven plagues' that John the Beloved outlined in the Book of Revelation. I have called this meeting today to let you know that these plagues have begun."

The congregation was surprised at his announcement, since Zion had thus far been spared from the affects of the first two plagues. The prophet opened his scriptures to the Book of Revelation.

"Let me read you John's description of these plagues. In Revelation 16:1 it says, '*And I heard a great voice out of the temple saying to the seven angels, Go your ways, and pour out the vials of the wrath of God upon the earth.*

"*And the first went, and poured out his vial upon the earth; and there fell a noisome and grievous sore upon the men which had the mark of the beast, and upon them which worshipped his image.*

"*And the second angel poured out his vial upon the sea; and it became as the blood of a dead man: and every living soul died in the sea.*"

The prophet then told the Saints about the swarms of horseflies that had killed so many people across Europe and Asia, and then he shared the reports they'd received about the oceans turning red.

"We've been sheltered so far from the plagues, but there's no indication in the scriptures that we'll be spared from any of the upcoming ones," the prophet said. "Let me continue in the scriptures. "*And the third angel poured out his vial upon the rivers and fountains of waters; and they became blood.*"

The prophet put down his scriptures and said, "I know that

this plague will directly affect us. We all understand the weather patterns, and through evaporation and rainfall our water supplies are soon going to be polluted. We need to take action. In a moment I'll explain the steps we're going to take, but first let me read to you about the fourth plague that will soon come. This one concerns me even more than the others."

He moved to verse 8 and read, *"And the fourth angel poured out his vial upon the sun; and power was given unto him to scorch men with fire.*

"And men were scorched with great heat, and blasphemed the name of God, which hath power over these plagues: and they repented not to give him glory."

The prophet paused, letting the magnitude of those verses sink in. "I have no idea when this plague will come, but I sense it will come suddenly, and anyone that isn't prepared for it will likely die. So at this time I request that the bishops make sure each home in Zion is stocked with at least a two month's supply of food and water. It is clear that the wicked will suffer greatly during this plague, but if we're ready, I'm confident we'll survive it."

The prophet then turned to one of his counselors and said, "And you thought we were done with food storage, didn't you?"

The Saints couldn't help but laugh. They loved the prophet and greatly appreciated his upbeat attitude no matter the challenges they were facing.

The prophet then faced the congregation again and said, "There is one other matter I would like to mention at this time. As you look at the wonderful apostles seated behind me, you'll notice that Elder Brown and Elder Negus are not with us. They've been called by the Lord to fulfill the prophecy that is also given in the Book of Revelation that two prophets will be in Jerusalem to help protect the city and to accomplish many other great tasks. They are already in Jerusalem and are fulfilling that prophecy, so the end is growing near, but we're not there yet."

✦ ✦ ✦

Following the broadcast, the Saints immediately got to work fulfilling the prophet's counsel. Containers of all shapes and sizes were filled with water from the abundant springs within the city, and large amounts of food were taken from each Bishop's Storehouse and placed in the homes of the Saints.

Within a week, the effects of the third plague became evident. The biggest attraction in New Jerusalem soon became the Missouri River, which began flowing bright red. Everyone within a few miles made the effort to see it with their own eyes. Other small tributaries also turned red, and even natural springs were slightly affected, but within a few days they became clear again.

The reports from the Cities of Light in the Rocky Mountains indicated that they were also faring quite well after heeding the prophet's advice and stocking up on their water supplies. Some of the Saints along the Wasatch Front said they actually preferred seeing the bright red hues of the Great Salt Lake and Utah Lake compared to their natural colors.

Meanwhile in Jerusalem, the Jewish leaders showed the apostles the ancient cisterns that were deep beneath the city. These were filled with clean water, and the Jewish people also passed through the plague with few problems.

The same couldn't be said for the Coalition nations, however. Although their scientists fully expected the minerals from the oceans to spread into other bodies of water, they didn't share that concept publicly with the world, hoping it would only happen on a minor scale. But nearly every river and stream across Asia and Europe turned red and toxic. Fear and panic spread quickly throughout the cities. While thousands of people died from thirst, many more thousands died from the violence that erupted as people fought each other for clean water.

After waiting for a few days, Elias decided to address the nations himself. The broadcast was shown in city centers and on all functioning television stations, reaching nearly a billion people.

Elias stood before the camera and introduced himself as the leader of the Coalition nations.

"I promise you that the clean water will return in a few days," he told the worldwide audience. "So please be kind to each other and help each other, and soon the water will return to normal."

Elias then placed a container of red water on the stand in front of him, and while waving one hand to distract the viewers, he used his other hand to slip a solution into the container that turned the water clear. Then he picked up the container and drank from it. Across the globe, a billion people gasped in unison.

Elias smiled into the camera. "See? Just like that the water will soon be clean again. Have faith in my words, and have faith in your leaders. The human race has overcome great problems, and we will overcome this one as well. Trust in me, and everything will work out."

After the broadcast, Elias quickly disposed of the remaining water and the container. He didn't need anyone to discover that the water hadn't actually been contaminated. It had been pure water with some red food coloring in it. He had simply performed an experiment any chemistry student could have done, but the stunt had certainly worked like magic. Most of the viewers had never seen him before, but now he was the most talked-about person on the planet, especially when the water in the rivers and streams returned to normal two days later.

However, there was a curious problem in translating his name to the billions of people throughout the Coalition nations. The name Elias was surprisingly difficult to pronounce in some languages. For simplicity's sake, a Chinese television commentator started referring to him by a name everyone could say easily, and it quickly caught on with the masses.

The name was Gog.

CHAPTER 21

Several days later, Emma and Tad North were sitting on their back porch in New Jerusalem enjoying a quiet evening chat. His duties as the bishop had kept him busy ever since the prophet's announcement to stock each home in Zion with food and water.

"You've done an excellent job," Emma told her husband. "I know it's not always easy to distribute those items in a way that everyone thinks is fair. Some families seem to think they deserve just a little more than the others."

"Well, my counselors and I did our best," Tad said, looking toward the sunset. "I think everyone in the ward is in pretty good shape now."

Suddenly the western horizon seemed to light up for few seconds before returning to normal.

"What was that?" Emma asked. Then they both looked upward and could see swirling patterns of colored light dancing across the sky, similar to the aurora borealis that was often seen in northern latitudes.

Tad glanced back toward the setting sun, trying not to look directly at it. "The sun is definitely brighter than it was a few moments ago," he said. "That's strange."

Emma went into the house and told the kids to come outside and see the dancing patterns in the sky. As the sun set, the patterns became more lively, and the Norths and their neighbors gathered together in the street to view and talk about the spectacle for several hours.

By morning, scientists in Zion were reporting that the nighttime display had been caused by the sun unleashing a monstrous solar flare that had affected the particles in the earth's atmosphere.

However, what had begun as a scientific curiosity soon turned into a potential global nightmare. The afternoon temperatures increased at least five degrees for ten straight days. The scientists didn't have a clear explanation why this was happening, but they felt it was somehow linked to the solar flare.

Soon there were record-high temperatures well above 100 degrees Fahrenheit being recorded in most areas, having a devastating effect on plant life. The high temperatures came with strong winds, and several major forests across the globe were soon raging infernos. Entire mountain ranges went up in flames.

One afternoon Tad looked at an old-style thermometer he kept on the back porch, and the mercury was maxed out at 130 degrees.

The Saints all knew that the fourth plague had arrived, and they hunkered down in their homes. Some homes had air conditioning, but it was useless against such heat. Staying indoors was stifling, but being outdoors was worse. Direct sunlight actually felt painful. So during the day most Saints stayed in basements or tried to sleep, rising at night when the temperatures decreased slightly.

The plague was just as brutal on everyone from a mental aspect because it just went on and on. People would wake up to temperatures in the low 100s, giving them hope the heat had subsided, but by afternoon the temperature would have climbed even higher than the previous day.

So many people passed away from the heat in New Jerusalem that the Saints had resorted to family members digging shallow graves in a designated corner of their community parks and then dedicating the site at dawn, rather than having full-fledged funerals. In some ways, the heat wave was a final refining fire for many of the Saints. If they endured this final test without too much complaining, they crossed over into eternal glory.

✤ ✤ ✤

In the Rocky Mountains, Doug Dalton smiled at the irony of where he was now living. The endless heat had driven the Saints along the Wasatch Front to find cooler areas, and the logical spot for the Springville Saints was the Jolley's Ranch campground in Hobble Creek Canyon. The deep pools they had built to collect water during their earlier stay were once again filled with fresh water from the nearby mountain springs. They were grateful the springs hadn't ever shown any sign of red residue from the third plague. The Saints had used rocks to create seating in the pools, which they jokingly called "cold-water jacuzzis." Sitting in the pools three or four times a day really helped fight off heat exhaustion.

The Springville Saints didn't have any tents to live in this time around, but nobody cared. It was too hot at night to do anything but to lay on blankets and sleep under the stars. They had followed the prophet's counsel to stock up on enough food for each family for two months, so they had been able to still eat well.

Doug pondered the contrast of his recent stays in the mountains. The first time he had endured one of the coldest winters ever recorded, and now he was living through the worst heat wave in history. The Lord was definitely using the natural elements to mold and shape his Saints, and Doug was sure the prolonged heat was removing many wicked people from the earth.

Across the globe, many countries were still trying to recover from the third plague when they ran out of usable water to take care of their crops. Now with the relentless heat and drought caused by the fourth plague, these countries were facing major food and water shortages, and millions of people simply collapsed and died from thirst.

Throughout the heat wave, Elias had stayed cooped up in a subterranean palace in the Kremlin. The gates were all locked to keep out the thousands of people who had come to Red Square to beg for relief. He would occasionally sneak up to a tower overlooking the square, hoping the people had left, but the crowds just grew larger and the bodies kept piling up. The reports he received were staggering. Some estimates indicated that the tragic events since the start of the year had claimed more than 30 percent of the earth's population. It was hard to imagine that more than two billion people were now gone, but he had no reason to doubt the figures.

Countries near the equator had suffered the most, and Africa in particular was quickly turning into a death zone, where people either died from the heat or from the violence that had spread through the cities and countryside as gangs roamed looking for food and water.

As Elias returned from his latest trip to the tower, a familiar person was waiting in his room. Elias pretended to not see him, but Satan said, "I'm not a fool. You know I'm here."

Elias finally looked at him, causing Satan to laugh, which was the last thing Elias wanted to hear.

"What do you want from me?" Elias muttered. He took a deep breath, trying to maintain his composure. "I'm working it out. I won't let you down."

"Yes, it looks like you've got things under control," Satan replied. "Billions of people are dead, and most of the countries in the Coalition are falling apart at the seams."

"Do you think I don't know what's happening?" Elias shouted, his body weak from the relentless heat. "I can't control the sun. Once the heat subsides, the Coalition will regroup. Just leave me alone. Get out of here!"

Satan was not happy to be treated that way. He leaped toward Elias and pummeled him to the ground several times, crushing him like he'd tried to do to Joseph Smith in the Sacred Grove in 1820. Joseph had been saved through divine intervention, but Satan knew no one would be coming from heaven in Elias' behalf. Satan could kill him if he desired, but Elias was still too valuable to get rid of yet.

"Never speak to me that way again!" Satan shouted as he released his grip on Elias, who coiled up on the ground like a child.

"I'm the master here, and I always will be. I've made you who you are, and I can take everything away from you. Don't forget that."

"Yes, Master," Elias gasped. "I'm sorry."

The insanely high temperatures lasted for more than a month, causing a full-fledged worldwide drought and famine, bringing every aspect of civilization to a halt. There were plenty of clouds in the sky, but they didn't provide any rain. Life took on a primitive feel. The only thing anyone considered important was finding some water to drink each day. The only people actually tolerating the situation without overwhelming casualties were the Latter-day Saints and the citizens in Jerusalem under the apostles' care. The Jewish leaders had helped the people prepare, and they were spending most of their time in buildings near the water cisterns.

Everyone else on the planet had been unprepared, and it was too overwhelming for them. Areas that typically had high humidity were especially hard hit. The air felt so suffocating and steamy that it was difficult for people to even breathe normally. It felt like they were constantly inside a sauna, with nowhere to escape. The only chore of those who had enough strength to do anything was to move their deceased loved ones outside to the growing piles of bodies along the streets. The stench in these areas was horrendous, and it was a living nightmare for the survivors.

One morning Emma climbed out of bed and felt better than she had in days. She went into the front room and looked out the window at the thermometer hanging on the porch.

"Does it really say 78 degrees?" she asked herself. "Could it be true?"

She ran outside in her nightgown, and it felt so cool. She rushed back inside and woke everyone up. They were thrilled, but they were actually shivering as their bodies tried to adjust.

That afternoon the temperature didn't rise above 90 degrees, and dark clouds were gathering in the western sky. By evening, rain began to fall. Everyone came outside of their houses once again, giving shouts of joy and letting the rain soak them.

Tad and Emma laughed at their children as David and Charles did "snow angels" in the middle of their parched lawn. They got muddy in the process, but they didn't care. Soon a steady stream of water was running down the curb, and Leah sat right in the middle of it, letting it splash all over her.

"Oh, this feels so great," she said. Her brothers joined her, cleaning the mud off their backs and getting happily drenched.

Emma smiled at her kids and said, "I think this means the plague is over!"

CHAPTER 22

---✤---

A few weeks after the plague ended, Charles North stood on a small hill and looked across the valley of Adam-ondi-Ahman. He had arrived in the valley early that morning with the youth service group that would be helping make landscaping improvements in the valley. Service missionaries had been working in the valley for the past few years, but the valley was too large for them to handle everything themselves, so they gladly welcomed service groups to assist them.

Charles was happy that he had been able to convince David and Phyllis to come along, and he had seen them periodically during the morning working along a trail. It was clear they were falling deeply in love, and Charles hoped they would soon marry. He really felt Phyllis brought out the best in David.

Of course, Charles had his own selfish motives for encouraging their relationship. After sharing a bedroom with David his whole life, he had really enjoyed having his own room while his brother was on his mission among the Ten Tribes. Now that the brothers were sharing a room as before, David's piles of stuff were cluttering everything up. Charles secretly couldn't wait to have the room all to himself again.

Charles' group had originally planned to complete this service project a couple of months earlier, but the effects of the fourth plague had forced them to postpone the trip. Although the plague's effect hadn't been as severe in New Jerusalem as it had been in other parts of the world, it had still been horrific. On the bus trip to the valley, Charles had noticed that most of the trees and grasses along the road were brown, as if everything had been baked. So he had expected to find the valley's foliage in the same lifeless condition, but the valley had survived the plague very well. Many flowers were now in bloom, and the leaves on the trees were green. It really was a testament to the group that the Lord had protected the valley during the heat wave.

During his lunch break, Charles retrieved his scriptures from his backpack. He had thoroughly studied the history of the valley, as well as the great event that awaited it, but it always inspired him to read the description of the first great meeting that had taken place there thousands of years earlier at the end of Adam's life.

He turned to Doctrine and Covenants 107:53-56 and read, "*Three years previous to the death of Adam, he called Seth, Enos, Cainan, Mahalaleel, Jared, Enoch and Methuselah, who were all high priests, with the residue of his posterity who were righteous, into the valley of Adam-ondi-Ahman, and there bestowed upon them his last blessing.*

"*And the Lord appeared unto them, and they rose up and blessed Adam, and called him Michael, the prince, the archangel.*

"*And the Lord administered comfort unto Adam, and said unto him: I have set thee to be at the head; a multitude of nations shall come of thee, and thou art a prince over them forever.*

"*And Adam stood up in the midst of the congregation; and, notwithstanding he was bowed down with age, being full of the Holy Ghost, predicted whatsoever should befall his posterity unto the latest generation.*"

Charles paused to look out across the valley, and he could easily envision it filled with all of Adam and Eve's righteous posterity. Then he flipped over a few pages to D&C 116:1 and read, "*Spring Hill is named by the Lord Adam-ondi-Ahman, because, said he, it is the place where Adam shall come to visit his people, or the Ancient of Days shall sit, as spoken of by Daniel the prophet.*"

Several latter-day prophets had spoken in detail about that upcoming meeting, which would be similar to the first one many centuries earlier. However, this second meeting would be even larger and would include priesthood leaders from all the earth's dispensations, who would report on their stewardships and return their priesthood keys—the so-called "keys of the kingdom"—to the rightful heir Jesus Christ, the King of Kings.

Charles closed his scriptures and looked around for his brother. He spotted him about fifty yards away, where David and Phyllis were still fully focused on one project—each other. They were sitting on a blanket eating their lunches, but they spent more time teasing each other than actually eating.

The service project went really well and the group cleared a large area where wooden benches would later be installed for the great meeting. As the sun began to set, the day concluded with a short meeting where the missionaries thanked the group for their help and explained once again the sacredness of the valley. The group members could really feel the Spirit, and many of them stood and bore their testimonies. Phyllis was among them, sharing the story of her conversion, and how grateful she was to be a member of the Church.

As the group prepared to get back on the bus and return to their homes, David pulled Phyllis aside. To her surprise, he knelt on one knee in front of her and held a small box toward her while saying, "I'm sorry that I'm so awkward about these things, and I've been trying to get up my courage all day, but I can't imagine getting back on the bus without doing this. You're so wonderful and I want to make sure we're together forever. Will you marry me?"

Several other group members had stopped to watch them, and Phyllis was a little flustered, but she finally smiled. "Your sense of romantic timing needs some work, but yes, I'll marry you."

The bystanders clapped their approval, and David opened the box and placed a small diamond ring on her finger, then he gave her a kiss.

Charles was already on the bus, but he opened a window and asked, "What's going on?"

A girl called out, "Your brother just proposed to Phyllis."
Charles grinned. "It's about time!"

Short engagements were the norm in New Jerusalem, because
weddings were purposely kept simple without a lot of frills. So
once a couple decided to get married, there wasn't much reason to
wait around.

So three weeks later David and Phyllis were gathered in the
New Jerusalem Temple along with several family members and
friends. As part of their special day, Phyllis had made a request.

"I want my family to be there, too," she had told David a couple
of days after they were engaged. He wasn't sure what she was saying,
but then she clarified what she meant. "Let's get their temple work
done in time so that if they're ready in the Spirit World, they can
attend the sealing."

"That's a wonderful idea," David said. "I'm sure they would
greatly appreciate that."

Phyllis had already completed the baptisms a few weeks
earlier for her parents, her brother and sister, and both sets of
her grandparents, but she had been waiting to do the rest of their
temple work when she would be able to be in attendance. Tad and
Emma had taken care of the initiatory work for Phyllis' relatives
the day before, so when Phyllis received her own endowments on
the morning of the sealing, members of David's family could serve
as proxies for her relatives in the same session.

There was definitely a tender spirit felt throughout the temple
session that carried into the Celestial Room afterward, and at times
the feeling of joy had been nearly overpowering.

Off to one side of the Celestial Room was a beautiful sealing
room, where the group now gathered. Waiting inside the room
was Elder Smith of the Quorum of the Twelve. He shook hands
with everyone as they entered the room, and once everyone was
seated, he stood before them and said, "It's a great privilege to be
here today to seal these two wonderful young people together for

eternity. I have dear friends in this room who have made sacrifices throughout their lives for the gospel's sake. Not long ago I was able to spend time with David's uncle Doug during some leadership meetings in the Salt Lake Temple, and he's a great man. I know his thoughts are with you today.

"I also want to acknowledge Sister Kim Brown here with us. I greatly admire both Sister Brown and her husband Elder Joshua Brown. We got to know each other when they were serving in Guatemala, and they have served faithfully ever since. As you know, Elder Brown is now performing a great task in the city of Jerusalem, and our prayers are with him. Of course, I realize if he could've been here, you would've chosen him to perform this sealing instead of me!"

His comment brought chuckles from the group. "But that's all right," he added. "Thank you for the opportunity. I'm honored to be here."

Elder Smith then invited David to escort Phyllis to the altar in the center of the room, where the couple knelt across from each other. The apostle gave them a few words of advice on how to have a happy marriage, and then he started the sealing ceremony. But after just a few sentences he stopped and paused for nearly a minute. Everyone sat still, wondering what was happening.

Elder Smith finally said, "I'm sorry, but there are other people here in the room that would like to be acknowledged. Phyllis, I know somewhat of your circumstances, and I want you to know your family is here with us today. They are excited for you and they want to thank you and David's family for helping them progress in the Spirit World. They love you and will be watching over you."

Phyllis burst into tears, and there wasn't a dry eye in the room. The veil between worlds was extremely thin at that moment.

It took a couple more minutes for everyone to compose themselves, then Elder Smith said, "Okay, I'll stop interrupting myself. We really need to get you two sealed! Let's proceed."

❖ ❖ ❖

Kim Brown's experience in the temple that day had left her feeling refreshed. Josh had been in Jerusalem for about a year now and she missed him terribly, but attending the endowment session and the sealing had reminded her that she would be with him throughout eternity.

The fact that Phyllis' relatives had been in the temple had also helped confirm to her that the hundreds of hours she had devoted to her own family's genealogical project during the past few months truly was worth the effort. She would be forever grateful to the wonderful Guatemalan sisters who lived nearby and had graciously taken turns watching the twins several times a week while Kim entered the names into the computer.

She was getting very close to completing the project, and so for the next few evenings she would put the twins to sleep and get back on the computer. It was a strange feeling inside her head. At first it had felt like her brain was crammed with information, but now there were fewer and fewer names rattling around in there. At last she typed in the final name and date in her mind. The woman had been born in Peru in 1162 A.D., the wife of one of the founders of the Inca civilization.

For the first time in several months, Kim's mind felt normal again. Out of curiosity, she checked her database to see how many individuals she had entered in since beginning the project: 32,065.

"Holy cow, that's a lot of names," she said. When she had been in the Spirit World with Tina in the ampitheater, it had looked like about 30,000 people had been there, so that estimate had been pretty accurate.

While in the temple, Kim had told Tad and Emma about the project, and Tad was eager to have his ward members help complete the temple work. The Guatemalan Saints also wanted to assist her, so Kim divided the names into several groups and then sent them electronically to the temples that were nearest to the Norths' ward and where the Guatemalan Saints most frequently attended.

The next evening she put the twins in their stroller and took a long walk through the streets of New Jerusalem, stopping to say hello to friends and neighbors she hadn't really talked to in a while. With all of those names now entered into the computer, it felt like a huge load had been lifted off her shoulders. Sure, her husband was thousands of miles away and was probably in constant danger, but she felt a great appreciation for the many blessings she had been given. Life was good.

As the Saints in the Americas successfully battled against the effects of the fourth plague because of plentiful springs and occasional rainstorms, the rest of the world sank into deeper chaos because of the lack of fresh water. Lakes that had covered several square miles just the year before were now mud bogs. Major rivers that had flowed for thousands of years were now dry, partly because the people upstream had blocked them off to salvage whatever water they could.

Northern Africa was enduring huge riots, partly because the water in the Nile River no longer even reached Egypt. Entire cities had become combat zones as rumors of drinking water would send the masses rushing to that location. These rumors were usually untrue, and the frustrated crowds would violently turn on each other. There was even some unsettling reports that people were getting desperate enough to drink human blood.

The lack of food was also a huge concern. The plague had come at the worst possible time of year, causing nearly-ripe crops to wither away all across Asia and Europe. As the plague had continued, large migrations of people began moving northward. People expected that there might be water trapped in the polar ice caps, but the ice was still thousands of miles away, and most people died during the journey.

Modern technology and communication had ceased to exist among average citizens. When the plague had first started, people had been able to trade their big-screen televisions, computers and DVDs for food, but now a loaf of bread was much more valuable than any collection of electronic equipment. Cell phones were a common sight laying broken in the roadways where people had tossed them aside as useless chunks of plastic.

In many ways, the conditions of the world had slipped below the standard of living of the Middle Ages. Without water, no one was taking a bath, and the stench that arose from raw sewage combined with the unwashed people themselves made it hard to even take a deep breath. Illnesses became rampant, and it was difficult for people to sleep at night because of the constant sound of coughing coming from every room in every building. Sadly, one particular ailment was growing increasingly common—thousands of people simply went insane and wandered the streets babbling to themselves, unable to cope with the overwhelming challenges.

In Moscow, hordes of people kept coming to the city from the south, expecting to find better conditions there. They were sorely disappointed, because the city had already been ransacked. Of course, there was one place in Moscow where there was plenty of food and water stored, but the Kremlin was now heavily guarded. Anyone who even hinted at trying to scale the walls was immediately shot by the guards who were watching over Red Square.

Inside the Kremlin, Elias felt like a caged tiger. He was growing more angry each day as reports rolled in about the devastation throughout the Coalition countries. He had been able to maintain some communication with each country, but he was starting to feel like he was now in charge of several Third World countries rather than a collection of superpowers.

Some of the other leaders were so discouraged that they called for the Coalition to disband, since none of the countries had enough resources to even help their own people, much less assist anyone else. Elias told them he completely understood, but he asked them to at least keep the basic organization intact.

"Have patience," Elias pleaded with the other leaders. "Winter is coming soon, and the rains will return. It will take some time, but we'll get modern society running again."

Elias maintained that confident approach in public, but he admitted to himself it would take at least a year or more to even begin to get the countries back on track. It was a situation where it was easy to be cynical.

"At least all of the mass starvations will reduce the number of people who need to be governed," he said to himself, shaking his head.

TWO YEARS LATER

CHAPTER 23

Josh Brown stepped out from behind a pillar and into the autumn sunlight as he looked up at the towering walls of the nearly completed Jerusalem Temple. The temple's construction had faced prolonged interruptions during the past two years because of the effects of the worldwide plagues, but the Jewish people had moved steadily forward on the project.

The apostles had helped with the construction in many ways, such as lifting heavy beams through the power of the priesthood, since there wasn't any fuel available to run heavy machinery. The outside stone walls had gone up rather quickly, but the intricate interior work, with amazingly detailed woodwork and finely crafted furniture, had taken the most time to finish. The craftsmen needed a few more weeks before everything would be completed. The wait would be worth it, though. The temple was a beautiful testament to the faith of the Jewish people.

The Jews had recently celebrated the Passover, and the apostles had also conducted a special service on Easter Sunday that was attended by several hundred people. The apostles had shared the gospel message with many families over the past two years. They had baptized about 500 people into the LDS Church and organized a ward.

At first, some of the Jewish rabbis objected to the apostles preaching and baptizing within the city, but Benjamin Cohen had intervened in their behalf, saying it was a person's basic right to choose their own religion. As he told the apostles, "Maybe I should get baptized into your church. It seems a Jewish Mormon will have twice the chance of making it into heaven as the rest of us!"

The apostles could have baptized many more people who were strong believers in the miracles they had performed, but the apostles only baptized those people who truly studied the gospel and gained a firm testimony of Jesus Christ.

The apostles spent many hours over the past months talking to Benjamin Cohen and the other Jewish leaders about LDS beliefs, and in many ways Benjamin was already converted to the gospel. He even believed that Jesus Christ was a divine being and that the apostles were able to accomplish their amazing miracles because of him. After all, Benjamin had heard many times when one of the apostles had commanded a miracle to happen in the name of Jesus Christ, and it happened every time!

A highlight for the apostles was working with men who had joined the Church and been ordained to the Aaronic Priesthood. The apostles had discussed with Benjamin Cohen a prophecy given to Joseph Smith in D&C 13 that indicated sacrificial offerings to the Lord would be made in the temple after it was dedicated.

Benjamin mentioned that there were Jewish prophecies that spoke of the same thing, and so he and other Jewish leaders had been teaching these men their duties and how to perform those offerings.

Josh thought about the three years he'd spent in Jerusalem. The first year had been a whirlwind of activity dealing with the effects of the four plagues. Many of the Jewish people had been killed by the plagues, but he and Colton had been instrumental in saving thousands of lives through healing blessings.

Another way they'd saved lives was by using the priesthood to command the elements to send rain showers over Israel every few nights. The clouds would form to the west over the Mediterranean Sea, drop their moisture over Israel, and then vanish before reaching Lebanon or Syria. It was a great blessing to the people and had allowed them to grow abundant crops and remain healthy.

✢ ✢ ✢

Josh shook his head to bring himself back into the present, remembering that Colton had gone back to their small home to prepare their lunch. As Josh turned to go eat, he felt someone at his side. He glanced over to see John the Beloved standing there.

"Hello! I'm glad to see you," Josh said. "I was wondering if you'd forgotten about us!"

"Not at all," John said. "You've both been doing so well that my visits weren't necessary. But I do want to update you on what's happening in the world."

"That would be great," Josh said. "I was on my way to meet Elder Negus for lunch. Would you like to join us?"

"Certainly," John replied. "By the way, the temple looks wonderful, and you've kept everything nicely watered. Good job."

They walked to the house, and Josh called out, "Elder Negus, we have a special visitor. I don't know if he's hungry, though."

Colton had just finished making soup and sandwiches, and when he saw John he jokingly said, "I've been told even translated beings can't resist my cooking."

John laughed. "They do look good, but really, I'm fine. You two go ahead and eat."

After a short blessing on the meal, Colton asked, "Can you give any guidance on how to prepare for what is coming?"

"Well, you know the timetable," John said.

Josh nodded. He had read the Book of Revelation so many times in the past three years that he had it almost memorized. He said, "*And I will give power unto my two witnesses, and they shall prophesy a thousand two hundred and threescore days,*" quoting John's own writing in Revelation 11:3. "We've been here more than three years, that only leaves a few months left."

"That's correct," John said.

"Then when will the fifth plague happen?" Colton asked. "We've been expecting it for more than a year now."

"It's coming soon, but the first four plagues were so devastating to most of the earth that sending the fifth plague soon afterward would've completely finished off the Coalition nations. This pause in the plagues is the Lord's way of giving the inhabitants of the earth one more chance. He wants to see whether their suffering has been enough to turn their hearts to righteousness."

"Is it working?" Josh asked.

"In a few areas, but most people either believe God has abandoned them or they blame him for their problems. The Coalition is using the common anger of the people to unite and strengthen them in preparation to conquer the world. As you can guess, one person in particular wants to destroy you."

"Elias," the apostles said in unison.

"Yes. Another attack is coming, but just follow the Spirit and you'll know how to respond."

"That's all we can do," Colton said. "On another subject, how is everything going in Zion?"

"Very well. The Saints who returned to the cities in the Rocky Mountains are prospering and millions of people live there now. Their standard of living is higher than before the Coalition invasion. The Cities of Light have spread across North and South America, and nearly all of the temples are fully operating."

"What about my Siberian friends?" Josh asked. "I would suppose their baptismal rate has been pretty high."

The members of the Ten Tribes that you led to New Jerusalem have all finally joined the Church," John said. "There were a few holdouts from some of those isolated tribes that joined us along the way, but the Spirit touched their hearts and they are all solid converts now. The tribes have been organized into hundreds of stakes, all with leaders from their own people. It's an amazing thing."

"I'm excited to hear that," Josh said. "We've been so preoccupied here trying to gain a few hundred Jewish converts that I sometimes forget about the incredible growth happening across the ocean. Most importantly, how are our wives and kids doing?"

"I knew that question would come up, so I checked in on them yesterday," John said. "Kim has been working on a big family history project for her Peruvian ancestors for most of the time you've been here, so along with taking care of the twins, she's definitely staying busy."

Josh got a little choked up. "I miss them so much."

John turned to Colton. "Cindy has also had her hands full with your active bunch, and some of them are as tall as you now. She's serving on the Church's general board over physical fitness and athletics, and she loves it. Many of her ideas have been adopted throughout the Church. The women in Zion are in better physical shape than they've ever been."

"How about the men?" Colton asked. "You'd think the plagues might have helped them slim down a little."

"Let's just say they're making progress," John said with a smile. "But I want you to know how supportive the Saints have been to both of your families. I know you've wished at times they could be here with you, but they're prospering and happy in Zion. It's where they should be, especially with what lies ahead."

Later that week, Elias lay wide awake in his Kremlin palace, rehearsing in his mind the whirlwind of events since he had taken control of the Coalition leadership. The plagues had been a challenge, but he had handled each one the best he could, and his stature in the global community had grown each time. His position as the leader of the Coalition was undisputed, and as the nations of the earth slowly recovered, he had purposely thrust himself into their everyday lives.

The term "Magog" had emerged among the general population to represent the Coalition, and it played off the nickname of "Gog" that Elias had obtained. So he didn't hesitate to incorporate these names into his unification efforts. The Coalition had distributed millions of large posters of himself that carried a simple but effective slogan:

Gog and Magog: Together we will succeed.

Along with having his face everywhere, Elias had printed millions of leaflets that told how much he cared for each person, and that they were each a vital part of the Coalition's rebuilding process. It was the same self-promotion techniques that had worked so well for other dictators in previous generations, but the people truly didn't see Elias as a dictator. Instead, he was becoming a messiah figure in their eyes who would bring them prolonged prosperity.

Elias had to admit his "I love each of you" campaign was working even better than he'd expected. Since he began this self-centered marketing blitz, there had been a remarkable drop in armed conflicts between regions. There were hardly even any local skirmishes. Everyone was just happy to actually have food and water again, and things were definitely looking up.

Elias had also effectively eliminated organized religion within the Coalition countries. During the plagues, many church organizations had ceased to exist, and he hadn't made any effort to help them reorganize. The church buildings were now called "community centers" where people could gather and hear Coalition propaganda, which in many ways sounded religious but didn't actually nourish the soul.

Elias was amused that most of the people considered him a prophet and a miracle worker. He hadn't actually performed any miracles, but that one televised trick when he had purified the red water had grown to mythical proportions. To capitalize on that, he was continually sending out teams of young people who were trained to promote the power of Gog. They would work their way through major cities and spread rumors of Gog's amazing talents and the miracles he could perform. As the stories of his latest miracles were spread by word of mouth, they would eventually become fact to everyone. Thus Elias became a miracle worker without really having to demonstrate it.

Elias realized the current peace among the nations was partly a product of the previous Coalition tactics. The people were conditioned to expect the Coalition to use force to halt any uprisings, so they assumed that if they stepped out of line, Gog would swoop down and crush them. The irony was that the Coalition currently had no army to speak of, but Elias felt it was best if the general population didn't know that.

He did plan to create another army once the nations were better stabilized, and his long-term goals still included conquering Israel, the only remaining holdout among all of the European and Asian nations. The British Isles had wisely joined the Coalition the previous year, and they were now rebounding nicely.

Elias also hadn't forgotten about North and South America. He knew the Americans had been strong enough to defeat the Coalition army, but he expected they had suffered from the plagues as much as the Coalition nations had. He recently ordered a team of scientists to attempt to link up with any satellites over America so he could receive information on the situation there, and he hoped they would get it working soon.

Either way, he felt that once the Coalition was strong again, they would be able to eliminate the Americans simply by outnumbering them. Despite the millions of deaths that had occurred throughout Asia, Europe, and Africa, there were still millions more people who were being carefully indoctrinated to the concept of Gog and Magog.

Elias had studied the teachings of many religions throughout his life, and when the terms "Gog and Magog" began to emerge as a description of him and the Coalition nations, the words had struck a chord with him. He knew he'd heard them before, and he tracked them down in a book known as the Bible. In that book a prophet named Ezekiel had foretold of a great leader named Gog emerging from the north countries with an army so numerous the soldiers would be like a cloud covering the land. The prophecy even specified that this army would attack Israel.

Elias was fascinated by the prophecy and the fact he was the fulfillment of it, but he could only laugh when he read Ezekiel's prediction that Israel would somehow defeat the armies of Gog.

"Sorry, Ezekiel, that prophecy won't be fulfilled," Elias said to himself. "But I have to give the Jews credit. They always keep a positive attitude even in the face of destruction."

✤ ✤ ✤

Elias smiled as he finally drifted off to sleep, feeling content with the direction the Coalition was headed. Yes, it was basically the old Communist system under a different name, but it was bringing security and happiness to millions of people who hadn't expected to even survive through the previous year. Now they had hope again in their lives.

"The funny thing is that I'm not really a people person, yet all of these people adore me," he said to himself. "God has been replaced by Gog. It couldn't be working out any better."

CHAPTER 24

─────────✣─────────

Kim Brown placed a large cardboard box filled with temple ordinance cards on her kitchen table. She had just retrieved the box from Emma North, who had helped coordinate the temple work for Kim's Peruvian ancestors. Emma had collected these cards from her ward members once all of the ordinances were completed. Kim still needed to pick up a similar box from Sister Mendoza, her friend in the Guatemalan ward who had performed the same service. She was so grateful for the willingness of so many Saints to help her complete the project.

Kim knew that all of the names were recorded in the Church's computer database, but with nearly 32,000 names being processed, it was difficult to check how the work was progressing. Collecting the cards had made it easier for her to make sure everyone's work was being done. She didn't want anyone to be overlooked and left waiting in Spirit Prison while the rest of their relatives had moved on to Paradise.

During her visit with Emma, they had marveled at the vast amount of work that had been completed. When all of the baptisms, confirmations, initiatories, endowments and sealings were figured in, more than 150,000 separate ordinances had been performed for Kim's ancestors.

"Wow, no wonder it took us almost three years to do them all," Emma said. "But our ward members loved doing the work. Hopefully they've had to build a new city in Paradise to accommodate all of the new arrivals!"

✢ ✢ ✢

As Kim got ready for bed that night, Emma's comment came back to her. She truly hoped all of those ancestors had moved across that Great Gulf in the Spirit World and were now living happily in Paradise.

She knelt next to her bed and prayed, "Heavenly Father, I know it is selfish of me, but if possible, please let me know that my ancestors are doing well in Paradise."

She stayed kneeling, fully expecting something to happen, but nothing changed. She finally climbed into bed, pulled up the covers and fell asleep, but soon she found herself standing in a field of beautiful red flowers.

She looked around and saw her sister Tina approaching her. "Is this a dream?" Kim asked.

"You're back in the Spirit World," Tina said.

"That was fast," Kim said. "After I finished my prayer, I felt a bit guilty about my request, so I wasn't counting on anything."

Tina laughed. "Well, it shows the power of prayer. At first, the heavenly council in charge of such matters wasn't going to allow you to visit again, but they soon switched their decision."

"What made them change their minds?" Kim asked.

"Well, I informed 32,000 people about it. Let's just say our ancestors got a little fired up, because they want to show you their gratitude."

"I'm glad to hear it," Kim said. "I'm eager to see them, too."

Soon the sisters were soaring above Paradise. Many cities passed beneath them, and Kim noticed she could hear a constant undertone of wonderful music praising Heavenly Father.

The overall beauty of the landscape and buildings was nearly overwhelming, but they didn't prepare Kim for the sight that loomed ahead. A mountain seemingly made of diamonds towered above them, and a majestic golden city lay below it, ringed by a fiery fence.

"This is where the Savior lives when he visits Paradise," Tina said. "Many of the modern prophets such as Joseph Smith and Brigham Young have homes there, too. They're all working together to prepare for the Second Coming."

Kim was still amazed by the beauty of the city as they traveled around the side of the mountain. On the other side of the mountain a slightly smaller peak was visible in the distance.

"That looks like the mountain I saw in Spirit Prison," Kim said. "Is that where our ancestors live now?"

"Yes, and they're eager to see you."

Tina guided Kim toward a spectacular city at the foot of the mountain. It resembled the design of the Inca city she had seen in Spirit Prison, but this city was built of white marble and literally glowed. Various exotic flowers and trees lined the streets, and at the center of the city was a vast temple pyramid surrounded by a large plaza, which was crowded with people dressed in white robes. They were all looking toward the sky in anticipation.

"What are they looking for?" Kim asked."

"You."

One of the people spotted the sisters and pointed them out, and a roar of shouts and applause greeted them. Tina guided Kim to the steps of the temple, and the crowd quieted down. Kim was humbled and touched to see them all wearing white robes, and their faces shined with the Light of Christ.

Nimhi, who Kim had met during her previous visit, stepped forward and took her hand.

"Sister Kim Brown, we want to formally welcome you to our city. We know without your efforts in our behalf, we would still be on the other side of the Great Gulf for many more years. We are so grateful the council has allowed you to visit us."

Kim nodded in appreciation. "I'm so happy right now. You all look so wonderful. The credit goes to the hundreds of faithful Saints in New Jerusalem who spent so much time to complete all of the ordinances. When I return I'll tell them how grateful you are."

Nimhi smiled with tears in his eyes. "We would appreciate that very much. We were permitted to go to the earthly temples to witness our work being done. Each one of us knows who served as our proxies during the temple work, and someday we hope to thank them personally."

Kim hadn't really thought about that aspect before, but it made sense that each of these spirits had been in the temple as eternal covenants were being made in their behalf.

Nimhi paused, still feeling very emotional. "We know it took a lot of time and energy for you to type in all of our names and dates, but as you look out at this large group, please realize that because of you we'll be able to be resurrected soon and be among the heavenly hosts that accompany the Savior as he descends to earth at the beginning of the Millennium. Without you, we would have remained in Spirit Prison during the Second Coming."

His words touched Kim so deeply that she couldn't speak. She simply raised her hand in the air and waved, triggering another round of appreciative applause. Finally she said, "If it's all right, I'd like to stay as long as possible and greet each of you. Please tell me your name and when you lived on earth. Believe it or not, I'm sure I'll remember it."

The crowd laughed, and they formed a line from the base of the temple out into the plaza. Kim spent what seemed like hours greeting each person and learning more about them. They expressed their excitement to be in Paradise and to be members of Christ's church. Kim was continually filled with emotion as she matched up the names she had typed in with the radiant, glorious people she was meeting.

As she talked with the final person in line—a beautiful woman who was Kim's great-great-great-grandmother—Tina motioned to Kim that it was time to return to her body.

"Just one more moment," Kim said. The entire group had stayed in the plaza, so she ran partway up the temple steps and called out, "I love each of you! Thank you for living such good lives while you were on earth, and for continuing to be wonderful followers of the Savior. I'll see you soon!"

Kim then took Tina's hand and they rose up above the city. She waved to the people, and then they popped back through the veil. As they entered Kim's bedroom, Tina said, "I don't think I'll be able to visit you again before the Second Coming, but never forget how much I love you."

"Don't worry, you're always in my thoughts," Kim said. "In many ways, I'm envious of you."

Tina was very surprised at Kim's words. "In what way would you ever be envious of me?"

"The Spirit World is so warm and inviting, particularly in Paradise. No one seems lonely. With Josh gone for so long, I've had my moments of self-pity."

Tina nodded. "I understand your feelings. I'm definitely surrounded by more family members than I could've ever imagined. But you have something I'm jealous of—true love. I've been able to follow your lives from a distance, and no matter what you're doing or where you are, your bond with Josh has always been so strong. Now you have the twins to make your commitment to each other even more solid. It's a remarkable thing."

Kim was quiet. She hadn't realized her sister might feel a void in that area, but Tina had died before she'd even had a real boyfriend.

Tina sighed. "I've been staying focused on my missionary efforts, since I realize I'll probably need to wait until the Millennium to really worry about anything romantic. Besides, I haven't met anyone on this side of the veil who I'm very excited about."

"I suppose the timing has to be right on the Spirit World, too, just like on earth," Kim said. "You'll meet the right person when you're supposed to."

"I know. Over here they like to remind all of us 'single adults' that the Lord has promised all righteous people will eventually receive all of the blessings of exaltation, including being sealed to a spouse for eternity. Thankfully I don't have much free time to fret much about it."

Kim clasped her sister's arm. "I have no doubt eternal marriage will be part of your future, and I'm sure your husband will be someone supremely magnificent—like yourself."

Tina laughed and gave her sister a funny look. "Thanks for the compliment. I do look forward to being married someday, and I want you to be at the sealing one way or the other!"

"I wouldn't miss it."

"Well, I'm enjoying this conversation about my non-existent love life, but you really need to get back in your body."

Tina gave her sister a big hug, then Kim found herself back under the covers, shivering as she had after her last trip to the Spirit World. But she also basked in the glow of what she'd just experienced. The magnificence of the Plan of Salvation passed through her mind, and she thanked Heavenly Father for granting her so many blessings in her life. She knew Tina would eventually receive similar blessings.

Tina's death as a teenager had nearly crushed Kim, because she had lost her best friend. However, now she fully understood Tina's passing had all been part of the eternal plan, and she marveled at what had been accomplished on both sides of the veil since that fateful day.

CHAPTER 25

A couple weeks later, Tad North received an early-morning message summoning him to a special meeting at the New Jerusalem Temple, and he was instructed to bring Emma with him. They reached the temple within an hour and quickly changed into their white clothing before entering the chapel under the center dome.

At least 20,000 people were already in the chapel, and the Norths found seats near the back of the room. The excitement in the air was almost electrifying. Something very important was about to happen.

A hush fell over the crowd and everyone stood as The First Presidency entered the room. The prophet went to the podium and said, "Please be seated. Thank you for coming so promptly, brothers and sisters."

Emma glanced around at the people seated near her. She recognized many of them, and as far as she could tell, this was a gathering of bishops, stake presidents and their wives from throughout the entire city.

The prophet continued, "At this very moment a momentous gathering is taking place about 80 miles to the north of us, and we've been invited to participate in this long-prophesied event. We first gathered you here so you'd be dressed in your white clothing and so we could travel together. After all, it's not often you see the Ancient of Days—even Father Adam."

A jolt of the Spirit raced through the room, and excited whispers filled the chapel. The prophet chuckled and waited for the noise to die down.

"I know you're all aware of the significance of the phrase Adam-ondi-Ahman, but in preparation for today's events, let me take a few moments to remind you of some key doctrines. Adam-ondi-Ahman means 'the land of God where Adam dwelt.' The prophets have taught that the Garden of Eden was located in this exact location where we have built New Jerusalem. When Adam and Eve were cast out of the garden, they settled in the area where we're now going—the Valley of Adam-ondi-Ahman. Just before he died, Adam invited all of his righteous descendants to gather in that valley so he could bless them.

"As you know, the Prophet Joseph Smith taught that Adam would again visit the valley in the latter days in order to preside over a great council in preparation for the Second Coming. At this council, all those who have held keys of priesthood authority will give an accounting to Adam of their stewardship. Then the Savior Jesus Christ will come and receive back these priesthood keys as one of the final steps to ushering in the Millennium."

His words took everyone's breath away as they comprehended the magnitude of what he was saying. The prophet got a little choked up and wiped his eyes. "I'm very excited to be able to attend today's events. We've been waiting a long time for this meeting."

Then he pointed to a set of doors on the west side of the chapel. "Most of the buses in the city have been obtained to carry us to the valley," he said. "Please exit quietly, and we'll see you there."

The crowd stood as one and reverently moved toward the doors. Everyone's faces beamed with excitement and anticipation. The Norths boarded one of the buses that became part of a large caravan on a highway heading north.

The caravan eventually left Zion's suburbs and began passing through fruit orchards. It was the beginning of the harvest season, and Emma saw large red apples hanging from the branches along the road. Later she noticed juicy peaches bending the tree limbs nearly to the ground.

The buses picked up speed, and soon the landscape was racing by. Everyone was silent, pondering what might happen at the upcoming spiritual feast. The only sound was instrumental hymns being played over the bus stereo system. The buses eventually came to a stop in a parking lot alongside a beautiful meadow. Farther ahead Tad could see rolling hills covered with lush grasses and beautiful flowers. He couldn't help but think of his son David's awkward proposal to Phyllis in this same spot, and he whispered, "Our son might not have great social skills, but he sure knows how to pick a location."

Emma smiled and took his hand as they quietly joined thousands of others walking up the road. They walked for about a half-mile before cresting a hill, and to their surprise they beheld an endless throng of white-robed souls already gathered in the long, sloping valley. A beautiful river flowed beneath the bluffs on the valley's far side, and every available inch of the hillside was filled with attendees.

"There must be a million people here," Emma said in amazement.

"There's probably many more than that," Tad responded.

A long wooden stage had been built at one end of the valley, and many dignified men in holy robes sat there. Hundreds of wooden benches had been reserved at the front for the group arriving from New Jerusalem, and the crowds kindly parted to let them reach the benches.

"Wow, why do we get the best seats?" Emma whispered.

"Probably because we're mortals," Tad answered. "Our eyes and ears don't work as well as the rest of the people here." He motioned to the crowds behind them.

"Are you saying they are . . ."

"Yes, resurrected beings," Tad whispered.

The Norths took a seat on a bench about thirty yards from the stage, where they absorbed the incredible spirit that surrounded them. Emma felt as if she could float.

Once the mortals were seated, an angelic choir on the valley's north side began to sing the hymn "Adam-ondi-Ahman," which fit the occasion perfectly. In crystal-clear harmony the choir sang:

The earth was once a garden place,
with all her glories common,
And men did live a holy race,
and worship Jesus face to face,
In Adam-ondi-Ahman.
We read that Enoch walked with God,
above the power of mammon,
While Zion spread herself abroad,
and Saints and angels sang aloud,
In Adam-ondi-Ahman.
Her land was good and greatly blessed,
beyond all Israel's Canaan,
Her fame was known from east to west,
her peace was great, and pure the rest,
Of Adam-ondi-Ahman.

Then the entire valley joined in the final verse. The ground seemed to shake as the vast congregation sang:

Hosanna to such days to come,
the Savior's second coming,
When all the earth in glorious bloom
affords the Saints a holy home,
Like Adam-ondi-Ahman.

Emma realized a strange sensation was taking place. The choir wasn't singing in English—but she understood every word. She looked at Tad, and he had noticed the difference as well.

Tad shrugged and said, "I suppose this meeting will be conducted in the Adamic language—the language of heaven. We are being granted the gift of tongues to understand it."

A heavenly peace settled on the valley as the song's words faded away. Emma watched the pulpit expectantly. A large, muscular man with white hair sat in the center chair, and she knew instantly that he was Adam. At his left was a stunningly beautiful woman who radiated joy — Eve, the mother of the human race.

Sitting at Adam's right hand was a man who could've been Adam's twin. This man stood and walked to the podium.

"That must be Seth," Tad whispered. "The scriptures say he looked just like his father, and he really does."

There wasn't a microphone, but Seth's voice somehow carried across the valley. "Welcome to this tremendous gathering," Seth said. "Father Adam presides here today, and he has asked that I conduct this meeting."

Seth took a few minutes to summarize the purpose of the meeting, which was to return the keys of each gospel dispensation back to Adam, who then would return them to the Savior himself in preparation for the Lord's millennial reign.

Following Seth's opening remarks, another dignified prophet—Noah—stood at the pulpit. He offered the opening prayer, pleading that the group would do the Lord's will that day.

Tad scanned the crowd and sensed a great order in the seating. The attendees were arranged by dispensations, with the priesthood leaders of the First Dispensation—which had begun around the year 4000 B.C. when Adam and Eve left the Garden—standing on the left hillside. Then the dispensations circled around the valley, and on the hillside to Tad's right were priesthood leaders he recognized from the last dispensation, which began with Joseph Smith and included all of the modern prophets.

It was a day filled with priesthood ordinances and ceremonies as the keys of the kingdom were returned to the Earth's first patriarch. The Spirit was very strong, and the Norths soaked everything in. Emma was so enraptured by the events taking place that she never got tired of sitting on that wooden bench. Thankfully Adam made sure the mortals were allowed to stand and stretch every once in a while, but she was stunned when Tad told her seven hours had passed. It had seemed like only three hours at the most.

The sun was creeping toward the western horizon as the transfer of priesthood power was completed. Adam stood before the group and wept openly. "The time is at hand, dear Lord," he prayed. "We have done what thou asked us to do."

He stood silently, then the most glorious being appeared at Adam's side. The mortal attendees gasped in surprise and awe, while the others in the crowd bowed in reverence before Jesus Christ, the Savior of the world. The mortals quickly followed their example once they regained their composure.

"I accept your offerings," the Savior said in a smooth, penetrating voice. His voice soothed Emma's soul, and tears rolled down her face as she lifted her eyes to see him.

The keys and privileges of the priesthood were returned to the Savior, the rightful heir. He then spoke to the group, eloquently describing the great millennial era that would soon come.

The prophet Abraham gave the closing prayer, and the Norths stayed sitting on the bench as the crowd began to disperse, not wanting the amazing feeling to pass. Then a regal-looking couple walked within a few feet of them, and Emma's jaw dropped.

"Is that Joseph and Emma Smith?" she whispered to Tad.

"Yes, I saw them on the hillside."

He meekly called out to them, and the Smiths turned their way. Joseph extended his hand, and Tad grasped it. He was pleasantly surprised that touching resurrected flesh sent a refreshing, warm spark through him.

Tad introduced himself and Joseph asked, "So your last name is North? Are you descended from Levi North?"

"I certainly am."

"He's a great man. He poured his heart and soul into building the original Nauvoo Temple. I appreciated his faithfulness and dedication. We still cross paths in the Spirit World at times."

Joseph looked past Tad's shoulder and saw Emma. "Is this your lovely bride?" he asked.

Emma stepped forward. "Hello, I'm Emma North. I'm pleased to meet you."

Joseph tilted his head toward his wife. "Do you happen to be named after my sweetheart?"

"Yes," she said, looking toward her namesake. "My parents greatly admire you, and I do, too."

Emma Smith smiled graciously. "I appreciate that, but we're all just part of the same Church, trying to do our best."

"What we've done is nothing compared to what you two did," Tad said. "You both sacrificed so much."

Joseph shook his head slightly. "We've been rewarded much more than we could've ever imagined, just as you will be. Keep the faith, my friends."

Tad and Emma spent the next hour meeting other faithful Saints, both mortal and resurrected. They all rejoiced together, knowing that the next time they would celebrate like this wasn't too far off—the Savior's Second Coming.

CHAPTER 26

On a distant hillside, Satan watched angrily as the events of Adam-ondi-Ahman unfolded. He could hardly contain his frustration as he looked at the prophets he had conspired against. He had turned entire nations against some of these men, and he had actually caused most of their deaths. Yet here they were in glorified, resurrected bodies.

He glared at all of them, seething inside. A long time ago in the premortal world he had ranked ahead of nearly all of them. He was the "Son of the Morning" and if everything had worked out as he had originally planned, he would be the one receiving the keys from them, not Jesus.

"Was my plan really that outrageous?" he asked himself for the millionth time. "It would have worked. I just know it. All I asked for was to be given the proper glory for all of my efforts."

He finally couldn't take it anymore. He felt he still had a chance to win this war, but it was up to his current earthly leader coming through for him. Satan rushed across the earth and found Elias just arriving in his Kremlin office.

Elias sensed Satan's presence, and he winced a little. Whenever the old serpent had shown up lately he'd been in an unpleasant mood. Elias really thought he could run the Coalition now without outside interference, but since Satan had helped him on his way to the top, he felt he needed to listen to him.

"It's time to step up all of your plans concerning Israel," Satan told him. "We haven't got time to waste."

"Hold on," Elias said. "Let's not rush things? We're making a good recovery from the plagues. Let's not jeopardize anything."

Satan rushed on as if he didn't even hear Elias. "Make it mandatory that every man over the age of 14 join the Coalition army. Tell them they'll be provided with food and shelter, and after the war they can claim inheritances in any country."

"Isn't that what the Coalition promised the soldiers who attacked America?" Elias asked. "That didn't work out. Maybe they'll decide not to join this time."

Satan looked at him incredulously. "What's wrong with you? Where is this doubtful attitude coming from?"

Elias sighed. "I'm just weary. We seem to have the deck stacked against us whenever we hurry into something. Why can't we just slowly rebuild first? Israel will still be there in a few months."

Satan nearly came unglued. "I won't tolerate any more delays or excuses! I'll get rid of you if I must and replace you with someone who will actually obey me."

"Hey, calm down," Elias said, suddenly worried Satan would fulfill his threat. "Please just tell me why you're so obsessed with Israel."

"Don't you understand?" Satan asked. "You've seen the satellite images as you've tried to solve the famine. Where is the one place it rains steadily?"

"Israel."

"Haven't you figured out why?"

"The scientists think that the Mediterranean Sea produces just enough moisture to cause that effect."

"Don't lie to me," Satan said. "We both know it's those two apostles creating their own rain clouds! Doesn't it bother you that their skills are so much stronger than yours?"

Suddenly Elias' weariness turned to anger. Those apostles had been nothing but a thorn in his side. He knew they created the tornado that had destroyed his army, and rarely a day went by that he didn't ponder how to get revenge on them.

However, without a strong army and all of the commotion going on in the world since that time, Elias had been forced to put his desire to kill them on hold. The Coalition was finally regaining strength, though, and the time had come for payback.

Satan was delighted by the change in Elias' expression, knowing he had struck a vulnerable chink in Elias' armor.

"They've basically been mocking you for three years," Satan said, stoking the flames of anger in his earthly leader. "They aren't superhuman. They're mortal, just like you. If you kill them, your troubles will be over. Just be sure to crush the Jews while you're at it before their temple is dedicated!"

Elias felt a renewed determination and purpose. "You're right," he said. "I never should have let those apostles grow so powerful. I can have 200 million men bearing down on Jerusalem within a month."

"Excellent," Satan said, suddenly feeling gleeful. "But what if the apostles somehow stop you?"

Elias gave him a fierce glare. "That's impossible. I'll kill them myself if I have to."

"That's more like it," Satan said.

Elias turned toward the door. "Excuse, me, Master, but I've got a city to destroy."

Nearing the End of Time

———— ✤ ————

With the Coalition forces being reorganized in preparation to crush Jerusalem, the final events before the Second Coming are quickly taking place.

Tensions are running high as the Jews rush to complete the temple in hopes of dedicating it before the imminent attack, and the Saints in America are watching anxiously for the remaining three plagues that will affect the world.

But it will be a joyful time as well, highlighted by the return of the City of Enoch, ushering in the millennial reign of Jesus Christ and 1,000 years of peace.

Read about these events and many others as the *Standing in Holy Places* series concludes in *Book Five: The Renewed Earth*.

ABOUT THE AUTHOR

———————✿———————

Chad Daybell has worked in the publishing business for the past two decades and has written more than 20 books.

The first three books in this series—*The Great Gathering, The Celestial City,* and *The Rise of Zion*—have all become bestsellers in both the LDS bookstores and the national retail chains.

Chad is also known for his other novels such as *Chasing Paradise* and *The Emma Trilogy,* as well as his non-fiction books for youth, including *The Aaronic Priesthood* and *The Youth of Zion.* He and his wife Tammy also created the *Tiny Talks* series for Primary children.

Learn more about Chad and the *Standing in Holy Places* series at his personal website **www.cdaybell.com**.